BLOOD MONEY

1948. Midwife Maudie Rouse looks forward to working with Llandyfan's handsome new doctor, Leonard Lennox, but is he all that he seems? When a young woman named Paula Mason turns up claiming to be his fiancée, this sets into motion a train of events that leads to her murder. The doctor is arrested, but the facts don't add up, and Maudie is determined to investigate. But could she be in danger of being murdered herself?

CATRIONA McCUAIG

BLOOD MONEY

A Midwife Maudie Rouse novel

Complete and Unabridged

LINFORD
Leicester

First published in Great Britain

First Linford Edition
published 2014

A catalogue record for this book is available
from the British Library.

ISBN 978–1–4448–2196–3

Published by
F. A. Thorpe (Publishing)
Anstey, Leicestershire

Set by Words & Graphics Ltd.
Anstey, Leicestershire
Printed and bound in Great Britain by
T. J. International Ltd., Padstow, Cornwall

This book is printed on acid-free paper

1

The street was deserted when midwife Maudie Rouse trudged back to the village shop. Half an hour earlier it had been filled with chattering children who'd been on their way home in the gathering gloom, but they were all indoors now, probably gobbling down their tea.

'Back again, Nurse? Forget something, did you?' The woman behind the counter put down her teacup and smiled. 'It's your age, I expect, dear. I know just what that's like. How many times have I gone into a room, only to ask myself what I was doing there? Just take your time and perhaps it will come back to you.'

Maudie swallowed her indignation. Mrs Hatch was a good twenty years older than her, if not more. 'I came in for a tin of Bird's custard powder,' she said. 'I got distracted by all those kiddies wanting their sherbet dabs and whatnot. Then when I got home I realized I'd have to come back again if I wanted custard with the apple tart I made this morning.'

'Ah, then you've had a wasted journey, dear. That custard's been on order for weeks, but can I get any? You'd think things would get better now the war's been over for three years, but no! Shortages and rationing are still the order of the day. How about having cheese instead? I can sell you a nice bit of rat trap. Goes down a treat with apple tart, does that.'

'I don't think so, thanks. I've got cornflour and vanilla at home; I'll just have to make the custard from scratch.'

Mrs Hatch leered. 'Got your young man coming for his tea, have you? That's right. You have to show him he's doing the right thing by wedding you, gal.' At the age of forty Maudie had recently become engaged to the local police constable, Dick Bryant, and it seemed that everyone in the village took an interest in their romance.

'No, he's on duty this evening. I thought I'd treat myself, that's all.'

'And a good thing, too!' Mrs Hatch

leaned closer to Maudie. 'Tell me, Nurse: what do you think about that new doctor, then? He's a sight for sore eyes, I must say!'

Now, in 1948, the provisions of the new National Health Act were slowly being implemented, and a young doctor had arrived in the village. Previously the nearest physician had been old Dr Mallory at Midvale, twelve miles away, an unsatisfactory arrangement that meant a heavy workload for nurses such as Maudie, who had had to deal with all sorts of cases in addition to her midwifery patients. Dr Mallory had been brought back out of retirement at the start of the war and was now approaching eighty.

'Dr Lennox seems capable enough,' Maudie murmured. 'And it's nice for him that he has his aunt to stay with. Better than being in digs, I'm sure. And she's let him set up his surgery in the old gatehouse on the estate, which will be handy for people to reach, especially with that bus stop just fifty yards down the road.'

'Handy!' Mrs Hatch sniffed. 'A sight too handy, if you ask me. I went up there with my bunions on early closing day, and the place was packed out. I couldn't even find a seat. Had to stand for three quarters of an hour!'

'It's only to be expected, Mrs Hatch. Until now people have always thought twice about seeing a doctor because it's cost money, but now it's all free they're taking advantage of that, and rightly so. Things will settle down in time, you'll see.'

'Hmph! All those young women — and some not so young, whose names I won't mention — are more interested in that handsome young doctor for his film-star good looks than for any medical aid he might be able to give him. There'll be trouble ahead, Nurse! You mark my words.'

'I don't think we need to worry,' Maudie said. 'A doctor can't get involved romantically with a patient. It's against medical ethics.'

'And another thing,' the postmistress went on, as if she hadn't heard Maudie. 'He's got a butler! What do you think of that, then?'

'A butler? Who has a butler?' Maudie

4

was confused by the turn the conversation had taken.

'I've told you. That Dr Lennox.'

'If there is a butler, it's probably Mrs Beasley's.' The doctor's aunt was a wealthy widow who lived on the estate that had belonged to her late husband.

Mrs Hatch shook her head. 'Oh, no, Nurse. He was right there in the surgery, all dressed up in a black suit, like an undertaker. Gave me quite a turn, seeing him there. We had to give our names to him and when it was someone's turn to go into the consulting room he announced them to the doctor.'

'Fancy!'

Maudie tried to make sense of this as she walked home. Dr Lennox didn't know the locals yet, so it made sense that someone should introduce each patient in turn. It seemed odd, though, that the receptionist, or whatever he was, should be a man; most doctors employed a mature woman, such as Miss Holmes, Dr Mallory's faithful dragon lady. It was essential to have a chaperone in the room when a doctor carried out an intimate

5

examination of a female patient.

Maudie knew she must find out more about this because people would expect her to know what was going on. She could, of course, call in at the surgery to see for herself, but having no plan to go out that way in the near future, she decided to drop in on her friend instead. Joan Blunt, the vicar's wife, usually knew everything that was happening locally — or at least, her husband did. She greeted Maudie kindly.

'Would you like a cup of tea, Nurse? I've got the kettle on.'

'No, but thanks for the offer. I mustn't hold you back when you must be wanting to get Mr Blunt's tea.'

'Oh, don't worry about that. He's gone out to see old Mrs Lester. She's dying for about the twentieth time and wants her hand held. I tell him he shouldn't pander to her so much, but he's afraid that the one time he stays away she really will pop off, and then of course he'll feel guilty. Now, how can I help you?'

'Mrs Hatch thinks that Dr Lennox has a sort of male factotum at the surgery. Do you happen to know anything about that? It's not just idle curiosity on my part, because people will expect me to know, and right now I haven't a clue.'

Mrs Blunt laughed. 'You've come to the right place, Nurse! We've already met the chap. His name is Bingo Munroe.'

'Bingo? What sort of name is that?'

'A childhood nickname that stuck, or so I understand. He was actually baptized Brian.'

'But who is he?'

'A cousin of Dr Lennox. In other words, he's another nephew of Cora Beasley.'

'But not another doctor?'

'Oh, no. I gather from her that he's not doing much of anything at the moment. He's been a bit aimless since he was demobbed from the army; trying to find himself, she says.'

'Or trying to find a job, more like,' Maudie observed. She knew how hard it was for men returning to England to find work. A young teacher at the village school had only recently returned to the profession he was trained for, following a stint as the school caretaker when there had been nothing else available.

'So Mrs Beasley has invited Bingo to spend Christmas with her,' Mrs Blunt said. 'Really, I do feel silly calling him that! It makes him sound like a dog. I shall stick to Mr Munroe in future. Much more suitable.'

'Doesn't he have a home to go to?'

'Apparently not. His parents are both dead, and he was an only child.'

'Do you know anything about the family?'

'As I understand it, there were three sisters. Cora married old Beasley, as you know. He was years older than her and very wealthy. Lettie is married to a prominent surgeon, and Dr Lennox is their son. Mona, Mr Munroe's mother, didn't marry as well. Her husband was some sort of clerk for the council, on the lowest rung of the ladder, I believe, and he died at an early age. He was gassed in the Great War and he didn't manage to hang on long after he came home. Through no fault of his own he left his widow and little boy in difficulty and I'm sure the poor woman had quite a struggle to support the pair of them.'

8

Maudie sighed. It was an all-too-familiar story. 'It's kind of his aunt to take an interest in him, then. At least he should have a good Christmas, staying with her. Nobody should be alone at this time of year.'

Later, standing at her cooker, trying to keep the lumps out of her custard, she counted her blessings. There were so many hard luck stories around, most having to do with the aftermath of the war, but she was one of the fortunate ones. In a few months she would be married to her fiancé, Dick Bryant, and they would be making a happy home together.

She wouldn't be altogether sorry to see the back of 1948. There had been another murder in the village earlier in the year and she had been involved in bringing the killer to justice.

She was looking forward to a year when nothing out of the ordinary would be happening — except, of course, for her wedding, which was something she'd never expected to see! However, it is just as well that we are not permitted to see into the future, for nothing would turn out as Maudie Rouse expected.

2

Maudie glanced at the paper chain she was making with some satisfaction. The strips of wallpaper, cut from a book of pre-war samples, were not as colourful as the shop-bought chains she recalled from her childhood, but the finished product would lend a festive air to the room. She only wished she'd been able to track down some proper glue: paste made from flour and water wasn't the same thing at all, and dollops of the stuff had landed on her apron.

Although she didn't have a Christmas tree she had managed to find a sprig of holly during her travels around the countryside, and she had propped this behind the studio photograph of her late parents. Christmas cards, depicting numerous robins and old-world scenes, were attached to the picture rail with drawing pins. All in all, the room looked quite Christmassy and the coal fire, when set alight, would provide the crowning touch.

Dick was coming to spend Christmas Day with her. He had to work on Christmas Eve but he'd been lucky in the duty draw and wouldn't have to go back until Boxing Day. Not that he'd be staying overnight at Maudie's cottage, of course. That certainly wouldn't be proper, even though they'd have separate rooms. She could lose her job in the blink of an eye over that! No, the poor man would have to return to his digs in Midvale. This time next year, though, they'd be safely married and all would be well.

Meanwhile, she intended to make Christmas Day a memorable experience for Dick. She had managed to get hold of a fat chicken that even now was sitting on the marble slab in the larder. Stuffed with sage and onion and accompanied by roast potatoes and Brussels sprouts, it would make a meal fit for a king. She could almost smell it now! She hadn't had time to make a Christmas pudding but Dick was partial to trifle, so she meant to make one of those.

Shuffling and giggling outside her door

alerted her to the arrival of young carol singers. She frowned as they gabbled their way through 'Once in Royal David's City'. Then they swung into the little ditty that signalled the end of their performance and the expectation of financial reward.

Christmas is coming,
the goose is getting fat
Please put a penny in the old man's hat
If you haven't got a penny
a piece of cake will do
If you haven't got a piece of cake then
God bless you!

'Oh, I'm not having that!' Maudie said aloud. She flung the door open, glaring at the assorted youngsters who gazed at her expectantly. 'What do you call this, then?' she demanded.

'Singing carols, miss!' a freckle-faced urchin informed her.

'Singing half a hymn, you mean, and then waiting with your hand out. Well, you lot, life isn't like that. You have to do a proper job or you won't get paid. I'm a midwife, you know. Do you know what that is?'

A tall girl nodded importantly. 'You bring the babies, miss.'

'That's right. And what do you suppose would happen if I brought the baby halfway out of my black bag and stopped, saying I want my money now?'

Giggles greeted this awesome thought and all at once Maudie's flash of temper subsided. 'Look, you'd better come inside. We're letting all the cold air in. Stand over by the window, all of you, and let me hear what you can do. Shall we begin with 'Away in a Manager'?'

When they had shuffled their way through two more carols, tunelessly performed, she placed a coin in a dirty little hand and sent them on their way, listening at the door to make sure they weren't up to mischief outside. Words wafted to her ears.

'Cor, did you see that? Stingy old cat! All she gave us was a mingy thruppenny bit!'

Maudie flung the door open. 'If you don't want it I'll have it back, then!' The youngsters fled.

Grinning, she returned to her handicrafts. If there was anything that annoyed her it was carollers who merely blurted out a few bars of song — one could hardly dignify it with the name of music — before rapping at the door, expecting payment.

Things would be different tomorrow night, when she intended to go to the midnight service at St. John's. The sight and sounds of the church choir, performing in the ancient candlelit building, would delight the heart and soul, calling to mind generations of the faithful who had worshipped here over the centuries.

Then they would all emerge into the frosty night, calling out to each other as they made their way home: 'Merry Christmas! Merry Christmas!'

* * *

Christmas morning brought with it an inch or two of snow. Maudie could smell it as soon as she brought her nose out from under the eiderdown. No doubt the shrubs in her garden would be sparkling with the white stuff and hungry birds, oblivious to the beauty around them, would be clamouring for scraps.

Her bedroom was freezing cold and, shuddering, she fumbled for her old Jaeger dressing gown that lay on the bedside chair. Putting one foot on the linoleum, she shrieked and drew it up again. If this cold snap lasted she would either have to wear socks to bed, or else take her slippers under the covers to keep them warm, ready for the morning!

By the time Dick arrived, his cheeks flushed from the cold wind, Maudie's cottage was warm and welcoming. 'Coffee?' she asked, waving the milk saucepan at him.

'If I can put a drop or two of this in it,' he replied, handing her a small bottle of rum. 'Happy Christmas, Maudie!' He kissed her on the cheek, like the dutiful husband he was soon to be. When they were sitting down he expressed delight over the sleeveless pullover she'd knitted for him. With any luck he wouldn't notice that she'd twisted one of the cables the wrong way, but it was at the back, under the armhole. She hadn't realised her mistake until she was making up the garment, and then it was too late to unpick it and start again if she wanted it completed in time for Christmas. Anyway, it was only a small error, and the finished product was a labour of love. Surely that counted for something.

'And this is for you,' Dick said, handing her a slim packet in holly-patterned paper. Tearing it open, she discovered a pair of nylon stockings, which was a prize indeed. 'Fifteen denier!' she cried. 'Wherever did you find them, Dick?'

'I got them from a chap in the trade,' he said, pleased. 'He's a rep who has to carry samples.' Seeing his eager face, she didn't tell him they were far too small for her. Possibly that was why the rep had given them away rather than passing them on to some female relative.

Somewhat ruefully she thought of her large feet, usually confined in her flat nurse's shoes. Talk about Clementine! Herring boxes without topses wasn't in it! Still, if she appeared perfect in dear old Dick's eyes, who was she to argue?

'I'll keep them for best,' she murmured.

While she bustled around the kitchen, checking on the roasting bird and boiling milk for their coffee, Dick sat at the well-scrubbed kitchen table, telling her all about Christmas at the police station. 'We've got old Josiah Jones with us again. It's becoming a regular event.'

'Josiah Jones? I don't think I know him.'

'No, you wouldn't. He's an old chap at Midvale; served in the Great War. Most of the time he travels around, sleeping under hedges and the like, but when the weather turns cold he prefers a bit of shelter.'

'Of course. Poor old chap.'

'Well, each year just before Christmas he heaves a brick through someone's window and of course we have to lock him up for a few days to show him he's done wrong. He knows we'll find him a bit of Christmas dinner, even if it is only fish and chips.'

'Cunning old devil! You can take him a chicken sandwich when you go back tonight; that's if you haven't polished off the lot by then!'

The day passed happily enough, yet Dick seemed distracted. Once or twice it seemed as if he was about to say something, but then he changed his mind.

'What do you fancy doing next?' she said at last, wondering what was up. 'Shall we go for a walk to get rid of the extra pounds we must have piled on after our dinner?'

'I don't think so. Hark at that wind! We'd get our heads blown off.'

'What, then? Cards? A game of scrabble?' Dick didn't answer. Puzzled, Maudie pressed on. 'Shall we have the wireless on, then? There might be some nice Christmas music.'

'If you like, love.'

'Dick Bryant! What on earth is the matter? You've hardly said a word all afternoon. There's nothing wrong, is there? You're not trying to tell me you want to call off the wedding, are you?' She was teasing, of course, so she was shocked when he looked at her with misery in his eyes.

'That's what we need to talk about, old girl. There's something you have to know.'

3

'Can you hang on while I make another pot of tea?' Maudie didn't really want another cup but she needed time to compose herself. Moving like a robot, she turned on the gas under the kettle and removed a fruitcake from its tin, ready for slicing. She had spent a lot of time worrying over that cake; should she put marzipan on top or not? She had no idea if Dick liked it. In the end she had used it, for how can you put royal icing on a cake with no marzipan underneath? He could leave it on his plate if it wasn't to his taste.

Now she had more important matters to think about. What if he was about to say he'd had second thoughts about their marriage? Should she keep a stiff upper lip and say she quite understood, or would she try to persuade him that everyone had pre-wedding jitters? It was a bit early for that, though. They hadn't set a date yet; the big event wouldn't happen for months.

A dreadful thought struck her. She didn't know a great deal about Dick's past. He was in his forties and she assumed that there had been other girls — women — in his life over the years. But had he ever been married and not told her? What if he were about to confess that he was still tied to some woman somewhere? Now Maudie understood how Jane Eyre must have felt when Mr Rochester's dreadful secret was revealed to her. Well, Maudie Rouse wouldn't be dashing off into the unknown with tears in her eyes.

'All right, Dick Bryant! Out with it! What is it you've come to tell me?'

'Where's the tea?' he asked plaintively. 'I was looking forward to a nice lump of that cake you made.'

'I haven't made the tea yet, and I'm not going to until I find out what's going on!'

'Why are you looking so annoyed, old girl? It's just a bit awkward, that's all.'

'So you're not going to tell me you have a mad wife in the attic?'

'What?'

'Never mind. Oh, for goodness' sake! Just spit it out, can't you?'

Dick leaned forward in his armchair. 'The powers that be have come up with a scheme where a team of bobbies will be sent to Canada for six months to study rural policing methods. It's supposed to be an exchange of ideas between us and the Canadians. Both sides probably have a lot of ideas to offer that could be implemented back home.'

'Oh, yes?'

'Well, the thing is, love, I've been selected to take part.'

'I see.'

'It's a real honour to be chosen, Maudie, and it won't do my career any harm at all. You know how hard I've been studying for exams, and promotion will definitely be in the wind if I do well at this.'

'I see,' Maudie said again.

'Well, tell me what you think.'

Maudie swallowed hard. 'Six months, you say. When do you go?'

'Steady on! I haven't accepted yet. Of

course I wanted to discuss it with you first.'

'Of course.'

'You're not being much help, Maudie. Please say something. Be honest, now. What do you really think?'

'It sounds like a great opportunity, Dick. Do you want to go?'

'What, miss a chance to see the world, all expenses paid? I've always wanted to see Canada. We've got cousins out there somewhere, you know. An uncle of Mum's emigrated after the Boer War. I might be able to look them up.'

Maudie nodded. Of course Dick should seize this chance, if that was what he wanted. She would be mean to stand in his way. But just where did this leave her? Would their wedding have to be postponed for another year, even indefinitely? What if he fell in love with the country and decided to stay over there? Worse yet, what if he fell for some Canadian beauty and forgot about the fiancée waiting for him in England?

'Then if this is what you want, you must grab it with both hands,' she announced bravely. If there were any tears to be shed she would hold them back until Dick was gone. 'When does all this happen?'

'Oh, not immediately. There'll be training courses to go on first, things like that. I understand that we sail at the beginning of April.'

Maudie noted that 'we'. So Dick had planned to go and had simply been waiting for her approval before he took the plunge.

'And it's for six months, you say? That means you won't be back until the autumn. That puts paid to a summer wedding for us, then.'

Dick scratched his chin. 'Well, that's the other thing I wanted to discuss with you. Why don't you come with me, Maudie?'

'What? I can't do that!'

'Yes, you can. We'll get married right away — at least, before we leave — and we'll sail as man and wife. Think of it, Maudie: a honeymoon on the ocean waves!'

'Are wives allowed to go along with their husbands, then?'

'Well, not as such.'

'What do you mean by that?'

'I mean no, that isn't the case. But there's nothing to stop you coming along as a private citizen, is there? We'll pay for your own passage and all that.'

'But would Canada let me in? I've heard they can be pretty sticky about letting newcomers in unless they have a sponsor over there.'

Dick laughed. 'You're not emigrating, old girl! Anyone can go as a visitor. We'll have to make enquiries, of course, to see how long you'd be allowed to stay, but that shouldn't be a problem.'

'But where would I live? You'll probably be staying in the police college or whatever they have over there. They won't let me over the doorstep. And if hotels over there are as pricey as they are here, that's simply out of the question.'

'I'm sure they have boarding houses or bedsitters there. Or there's always the YWCA. We'll think of something. And when I get time off we'll be able to see a bit of the country. Niagara Falls! Ottawa! Old Quebec City! What could be more wonderful? I realise I've sprung this on you, Maudie, but I want you to think about it very seriously. Will you do that?'

'I suppose I can do that, Dick.'

'Right, then! Now where's that cuppa and a bit of your cake?'

That night Maudie tossed and turned in her bed until her hot water bottle went cold. Then she had to get up to visit the toilet, thanking her lucky stars that, unlike many homes in the village, her cottage had indoor plumbing. She paused at the bedroom window and looked out. It was a very cold night and the sky seemed filled with stars.

If she had to boil the kettle to heat up the hot water bottle, she might as well make a cup of Horlicks while she was at it. Sitting in the kitchen with the oven on and its door left open for warmth, she mulled over Dick's amazing proposal. Brought up in modest surroundings, she had never even considered travelling aboard, and now she was on the verge of taking part in a marvellous adventure. She, Maudie Rouse, miraculously transformed into Mrs Bryant, would be a married woman, travelling in style.

Well, perhaps 'style' would be too elegant a word. As people with a modest income they'd be travelling in steerage, or whatever they called it nowadays, and what sort of accommodation would be theirs? A lot of the ocean liners had been adapted as troop ships during the war and it seemed unlikely that they had been restored to their former luxury so soon. And what if they didn't have shared accommodation? Dick might well be expected to stay with his colleagues, sleeping in a hammock like those soldiers who had been shipped off to war.

And Maudie had never been to sea and didn't know if she would make a good sailor. Some honeymoon it would be if she spent a week hanging over the railings, emptying the contents of her stomach into the Atlantic.

She was aware that she was being negative. Ten, twenty years ago she would have rushed headlong into such an adventure without a second thought. Now the steady practical streak that made her such a good nurse and midwife had come to the fore.

'You won't get any sleep tonight, my

girl,' she told herself, 'so you may as well look at the rest of it. You promised Dick you'd think seriously about all this, and that includes the negative side as well as all the exciting possibilities.'

4

In the New Year Maudie carried on with her regular routine, still not having come to a definite conclusion as to her immediate future with Dick. Nobody seemed to notice that she was rather distracted. Apart from the necessary talk connected with childbirth and its aftermath, her patients seemed to have only one topic of conversation, and that had to do with young Dr Lennox and the chances of getting him married off to some fortunate local girl.

On a crisp Monday morning Maudie called at the farm of Oliver and Alice Bassett, to see their married daughter. Mary Taylor, the mother of a strapping toddler, was now expecting her second child. Mary and her mother, like all the rest of the local women, were very interested in the doctor's private life.

'Whoever manages to snare that young fellow will have it made!' Oliver Bassett muttered, happening to pass through the kitchen in time to hear what his women-folk were saying.

'I don't know so much,' Maudie said. 'Being the wife of a busy doctor isn't all it's cracked up to be. He's likely to be called out at all hours and then there are medical conferences and courses to attend, never mind having to read reams of literature to keep up with the latest advances in medicine and methods of treatment. That doesn't leave him much time to pay attention to his wife.' A few of her nursing school classmates had actually married doctors and most of them seemed to lead lonely lives.

'Never mind all that!' Bassett told her. 'When old Cora croaks they'll be rolling in money.'

'Oliver, really!' his wife complained. 'Must you be so coarse?'

'What's wrong with that? It's true, ain't it? The old girl can't go on forever, and what's to happen to her money then, eh? Young Lennox will scoop the lot!'

'We don't know that, Oliver! There's another nephew, don't forget. That Mr

Munroe. Why would she leave him out? Blood is thicker than water, you know.'

'She might leave it all to the cats' home,' Mary said, laughing. 'Or we know she's in thick with the vicar. It could all go to the church.'

'And so it should!' Oliver was a churchwarden at St John's. 'You've seen the state of that roof, and the church fête was a complete failure as far as adding to the repair fund went.'

'It was hardly anyone's fault that we had that murder, Dad! Perhaps this year it will be a great success.'

But Maudie happened to know that there wasn't to be a fête in 1949. Mrs Blunt had told her as much. 'All that work for nothing, Nurse, and poor Madam Zora murdered in her tent.[1] I'm still having nightmares about the whole thing, and if I had my way we'd never have a fête again. Donald doesn't quite agree, but he does feel it wouldn't be the thing to hold another so soon.'

'Perhaps the vicar could make a direct

---

[1] *Blood Ties.*

appeal to Mrs Beasley,' Maudie remarked. 'Who knows, if she's as rich as they say, she might cough up enough to do the whole job.'

'Fat chance!' Oliver grunted. 'Tight-fisted as they come, is Cora Beasley.'

'Yes, well, I must be getting along. I'd like to examine you now, Mrs Taylor. Shall we pop up to your bedroom? And thanks for the tea, Mrs Bassett. That went down a treat on a frosty morning!'

★   ★   ★

Daisy Larke was another young woman who was expecting her second child. Her little boy, Richard, was a bit older than young Ollie Bassett, and now that he'd got over a spell of colic he was doing well. Daisy's curmudgeonly old father had come to live with the Larkes and he often made the girl's life a misery with his demands, but he had simmered down after Maudie had treated him to a few home truths. It had helped, too, when Mrs Blunt had arranged visits from some of the older church members, which relieved the loneliness he'd suffered following the death of his wife. He enjoyed a game of draughts or cards.

The old man perked up when Maudie came through the door. 'Here she is! She'll give us all the latest news!'

'You make me sound like a right old gossip, Mr Miller. What is it you want to know?'

'Why, what everybody's talking about, of course. There's only one thing that matters round here.'

'Not you as well, Mr Miller! I'm sure Dr Lennox is quite capable of finding a wife for himself without any help from us, even if he is Llandyfan's answer to Clark Gable or Gregory Peck.'

'I dunno what you're on about, Nurse.'

'Oh, sorry! What are you talking about, then?'

'Why, them new houses being built down on old Carter's farm, of course. Eyesores, that's what! And what sort of people is going to move in there, eh? It's asking for trouble, that's what I say, and you just wait — I'll be proved right in the end, when it's too late to do anything about it.'

'Carter? You mean the old gentleman who died last autumn?'

'That's him. He left the place to his son, only he don't want it and it's been sold to the council. Now they're plastering the whole place with them little doll's houses. I know that for a fact. Some of my mates have told me all about it.'

'Dad means those places they put together out of ready-made walls and that,' Daisy explained. Prefabs, they call them.'

'Glorified Nissen huts,' Fred muttered.

'Oh, yes. I've read about that prefabricated housing scheme the government is involved in,' Maudie said. 'It sounds like a good idea to me. So many people were made homeless during the blitz. They deserve somewhere nice to live now. And the prefabs are nothing like Nissen huts, Mr Miller. Judging by the drawings I've seen in the newspaper, they're cosy little places. Compact, yes, but quite comfortable. Anyway, I understand that they're only meant to be temporary. In a few years' time they'll be replaced by permanent housing, once building materials are freely available again.'

And here endeth the first lesson, Maudie told herself. She didn't mean to sound like some sort of socialist tract, but part of her job was to smooth the way for her young mothers, making sure that they didn't suffer undue stress. If she didn't succeed in patting down old Fred's feathers he'd work himself up to a pitch where poor Daisy would bear the brunt of his ire. He wasn't a bad man, but he did love the sound of his own voice.

'It's not the houses I object to,' Fred went on, as if Maudie hadn't spoken. 'It's the people in them. How do we know they won't be riffraff, eh? Traipsing in here from the big city slums.'

'I'm sure they'll be perfectly decent people, Mr Miller, and furthermore it will up to us to welcome them.' Maudie thought it best not to remind him that he was an incomer himself.

She could understand why people were worried, though. Llandyfan was a rural community, situated on the border between England and Wales. Nothing much had changed here for a very long time. The Norman church, the village shop, the local school would have been readily recognisable if some Victorian resident had risen from the grave to survey his surroundings. If new inhabitants suddenly flooded the community, would they bring change with them? Modern ways that were out of keeping with everything the local residents held dear? Her face must have shown something of her thoughts, for the old man nodded.

'Aye, you get it now, don't you, Nurse? And people ain't going to like it, not one little bit. There'll be trouble ahead, and I hope it don't lead to blows. Two murders we've had here in just two years, in a place that was peaceful as the tomb before that, even if there was a war on.'

'Ah, well, I suppose we'll just have to wait and see, won't we?'

'Some of us will,' the old man said, wrinkling his nose. 'You won't be around, will you, Nurse? You'll be running off with that chap of yours any minute now, and don't tell me you won't.'

'Dad!' Daisy looked embarrassed.

Maudie sighed. It had been too much to hope for that her engagement could be kept secret for more than five minutes. Any news of births, marriages and deaths tended to fly across country as if transported by carrier pigeon. As Mrs Blunt was often heard to say, there was really no need to take the *Midvale Chronicle* when the jungle drums were beating.

'Nothing is settled yet, Mr Miller,' she said primly. At least word of Dick's impending departure was not yet circulating.

'Well now, Nurse, if he doesn't come up to scratch you could do worse than wed me, and don't you forget it!'

Was he serious? Maudie frowned at the old man but he was bent over his newspaper and she couldn't read his expression. She looked over at Daisy, who shrugged. Yes, of course it was a joke. It had to be. It was so seldom that he came out with anything of that nature that it was hard to recognise when it actually happened!

5

Maudie's final home visit of the day was to Mrs Patsy Sawyer, who had recently given birth to a little girl with a mop of black hair. She wasn't happy about the baby, who seemed listless at times. The young woman came to the door, wiping her mouth with the back of her hand. Maudie guessed that she had just finished one of her favourite cream doughnuts.

Maudie could fancy one herself, but she usually managed to avoid the temptation, reminding herself that they went straight to her hips. Dick said that he liked a bit of weight on a woman — something to hold on to — but there was such a thing as going too far. Maudie couldn't afford to replace all her clothes if she went up a size or two, and that was all there was to it.

Patsy Sawyer was another matter. In vain Maudie had encouraged the girl to eat vegetables and to keep the fattening stuff to a minimum, but it was like talking to a brick wall. Patsy's favourite piece of kitchen equipment was the frying pan and she and her husband ate mounds of chips, the greasier the better.

'How is baby, Mrs Sawyer?' Maudie asked, following her patient into an untidy kitchen. She could hear the little one wailing in the distance.

'She's being a real nuisance. Just hark at that! I don't know what she wants. She's had her bottle but she just won't settle.'

'Shall I go and take a look?' Without waiting for an answer, Maudie went into the sparsely furnished parlour, where she found the child lying in a battered pram. She scooped her up and returned to the kitchen.

'It's too cold for her in there, Mrs Sawyer. See, her little legs are all mottled. And she's wringing wet. She needs a clean nappy.'

'There's one up there,' the girl said, pointing to an overhead rack that was draped with grey-looking garments. 'You change her for me, Nurse. I'm too tired.'

Sighing, Maudie placed the baby in her mother's arms, leaving herself free to handle the pulley attached to the rack. 'I'll do it this once, Mrs Sawyer, but you really will have to buck up, you know.' Some women genuinely did suffer from postpartum depression, and needed expert help. Clarice Allen, another of her mothers, was a case in point. Patsy Sawyer, though, was just plain lazy, or so it seemed to Maudie.

'Of course you're tired, Mrs Sawyer, with baby waking you up for the two o'clock feed. But give her a few weeks and then she'll start sleeping through the night, and you'll be able to get more rest.'

'Oh, it's not just that. I didn't know it was going to be like this, Nurse!'

'Looking after a newborn baby does call for a lot of patience.'

'It's not just that. It's everything! It's my hubby! He says I'm a mess! He wants to know when I'm going to get my figure back. I've seen the way he looks at that new barmaid in the Royal Oak! And he's started staying out too late instead of coming home to me and Dorena May!

Can you have a word with him, Nurse? Please?'

Maudie hesitated. She made it a practice never to interfere between husband and wife, unless actual abuse was involved. If she tackled the young man they'd resent it later when their disagreements had been cleared up.

'I think you'll find that your hubby will be more understanding when he gets used to being a father. Why not try to involve him in Dorena May's care? For instance, could he wheel her out in her pram on weekends when the weather is fine?'

'What! And let his mates see him? No fear! I know what he'd say! Kids are women's work, that's what. Never mind that, Nurse. What I want to know is, when do I get my figure back?'

'I did say that twenty pounds was the ideal weight gain in pregnancy,' Maudie said carefully. 'You seem to have put on forty.' *And that's a conservative estimate, but I mustn't be too hard on the girl. She has enough on her plate without being made to feel badly about herself.*

'It's just water, though, isn't it? Won't it sort of drain off?'

'I'm afraid not. You'll have to go on a diet.' Maudie repeated her advice about fruit and vegetables and cutting down on greasy fried foods and sugary pastries. Mrs Sawyer curled her lip.

'All right for some, isn't it? Just look at you, Nurse! You don't know what you're talking about. You're not in bad condition, really, considering your age. I bet you've never had to go on a diet, so don't preach to me.'

Count to ten, Maudie! 'It so happens that I pedal my way all round this district, day in, day out. That keeps the pounds off. You should try it, Mrs Sawyer. Get yourself a bicycle and learn to ride it.'

'And who looks after this one while I do that?' Patsy's expression was sullen. Maudie gave up. Let the silly little wretch eat herself to death if that was what she was determined to do. When Maudie returned to her little office in the parish hall she found a young woman pacing up and down, looking worried.

'Hello, I'm Nurse Rouse. Were you

41

waiting for me? I don't think we've met, have we?'

'I'm Celia Groom. Mrs Bart Groom, that is. I think . . . ' Tears rolled down her pale cheeks.

'You'd better come in,' Maudie said, unlocking the door. 'How about a cup of tea? It sounds like you could do with one. Then you can tell me all about it.'

Some minutes later, when they each had a steaming cup of tea in front of them, Maudie judged it was time to speak. 'Now, then, what have you come to tell me?'

Mrs Groom gulped. 'I think I have cancer, Nurse!'

'I'm so sorry to hear that. And what gives you that idea? Have you found a lump, for instance? If you have, you must see a doctor right away. I'm just a midwife. I can't diagnose serious illness.'

'No, I haven't got a lump. But I feel so tender here' — Mrs Groom patted her chest — 'and I've lost weight. My skirts have started to hang loose on me. And I'm so tired all the time.'

'Perhaps you do need my services after

all,' Maudie said cheerfully. 'People naturally think of putting on weight in pregnancy, but it's quite normal to lose a few pounds in the early months.'

'I'm not expecting, Nurse. I'm still having my monthlies, you see, although they're not very heavy.'

'There again, it's not unheard of for a pregnant woman to have some bleeding at the time when a period would normally be expected. But of course you should see a doctor to make sure that there isn't some other explanation.'

'I've seen a doctor.' Mrs Groom fumbled in her coat pocket and pulled out a damp handkerchief.

'Here, take this,' Maudie said, taking a clean cotton rag and a hand mirror out of her desk drawer. 'Your mascara's run. You can't go out on the street looking like that. Who was it you saw? Dr Lennox, perhaps?'

'No, we've only just come here from Midvale. Bart — my husband — he's just found work helping to put up the prefabs. My mother lives here in the village and we're staying with her for now. Dr Mallory used to be our doctor but he's

43

retired now. I saw the new man, Dr Dean.'

'Oh.' Maudie was well acquainted with Dr Dean and she knew that he was woefully lacking when it came to displaying a pleasant bedside manner. 'And was he able to set your mind at rest?'

Mrs Groom twisted her hands together on her lap. 'I told him I had a feeling I was expecting and I'd come to find out. We've been wanting so much to start a family, you see. But when he heard about the bleeding he laughed at me and told me not to be so silly. Didn't I know that sort of thing stopped when a woman is pregnant? He told me to go home and scrub a floor or something and not to waste his time again.'

Rage welled up in Maudie. As far as she knew the man hadn't specialised in obstetrics, but surely he'd had to take a midder rotation in his days as a medical student? He should be familiar with the basics. But that wasn't the worst of it. Her symptoms could also point to something sinister, which had to be investigated at once.

'And he didn't examine you, Mrs Groom?'

'No. I was so mortified I just ran out of there, and I'm never going back!'

'I see. Well, if you'll hop up on the couch there I'll certainly take a look at you, and then we must make an appointment for you with Dr Lennox. He's very pleasant. I know you'll like him.'

6

When her patient had left, Maudie picked up the phone to call Dr Lennox. After several attempts she decided there must be a fault on the line, because somebody should have answered at this time of day. She put on her coat, locked up the office, and marched up to the shop. Mrs Hatch was also the postmistress, and there was a telephone in the tiny kiosk where she dispensed stamps and postal orders. Maudie didn't want to waste time by going home to make the call, in case her line was also useless.

'Nothing wrong with my line here,' Mrs Hatch announced, when she had tried her phone. 'I'll call Faults, but it's probably only one of those dotty girls at the exchange, plugging in the wrong thing at the switchboard or something.'

'Then you'd better tell Faults to get on with it as soon as possible, Mrs Hatch. How are people supposed to get in touch with Dr Lennox in case of emergency? The phone at the surgery may not be completely out of service, you know. If they are able to call out they may not be aware that the rings aren't coming in.'

'I know my job, Nurse. I'll get on to Faults right away, although if you ask me it's all down to that Bingo person. He's probably left the phone off the hook.'

*　*　*

Too restless to return to her paperwork, Maudie decided it was time to make a call on Dr Lennox. The weather was cold, but it wasn't too bad for cycling. She'd enjoy a trip through the lanes.

She wanted to have a snoop round his surgery in any case, and while she was at it she would make an urgent appointment for Mrs Groom. He knew what his colleague was like, so she would have no compunction in reporting to him what her patient had said.

The gatehouse was a survival of the days when great wrought iron gates barred the entrance to the estate now owned by Mrs Beasley. The family who lived there had been employed to open the gates to admit approaching traffic, whether carriages, pony traps or anything in between. Bizarre though this seemed to Maudie, she sometimes wished that she had a servant to open and close farm gates for her when she arrived on her trusty bicycle.

The gates had long since disappeared and had never been replaced. In the early days of the war iron railings, gates and even pots and pans had been taken by the government to be melted down. Maudie wasn't sure what the end result was. Spitfires? Bullets? In any event there were no gates there now.

The gatehouse was built of mellow brick, with ivy clinging to its walls. Maudie opened the front door and found herself in what must have been the family's living quarters in the old days. The only furniture in it now was an odd assortment of chairs arranged in rows, and an old-fashioned table strewn with copies of magazines and children's picture books.

'We're not open now. Surgery hours are posted on that list on the wall there. You'll have to come back later.'

Maudie jumped at the sound of the sepulchral voice. She'd been so engrossed in taking in her surroundings that she hadn't heard the man's approach. She looked up to see a tall man dressed in black. This, then, must be the famous Bingo Munroe. As Mrs Hatch had said, he did look like an undertaker, gloomy expression and all.

'Oh, I'm not a patient,' she explained. 'I'm Nurse Rouse, the midwife.'

'Then you'll have to come back later. As I said, the doctor isn't seeing anyone now.'

'That's all right. I shan't keep him long.'

Bingo Munroe drew himself up to his full height, looking down his long nose at Maudie. 'My good woman, did you not hear what I said? Or perhaps the concept is too much for you to understand? Dr Lennox has finished seeing patients for today, and he's about to start his lunch. Not that it's any of your business. Now, do I make myself clear?'

Maudie looked him right in the eye. 'And shall I make myself clear? To begin with, I am not your good woman. And secondly, I'm here to see the doctor about an urgent case, and see the doctor I shall! Now then, where can I find him? Through here, is it?' She brushed past him and flung open the nearest door.

Unfortunately it turned out to be not the entrance to another room, as she had hoped, but the door to a boxed staircase. This was an old-fashioned enclosed stair with doors top and bottom, and walls on either side, holding a number of hooks for storage purposes. Red-faced, she took a step backwards, pretending she hadn't noticed Bingo's triumphant expression.

'I'll just . . . er . . . ' she began, but at that moment the upper door opened and Dr Lennox peered out. 'Oh, hello, Nurse. I was wondering when you'd call round. There are one or two things we need to discuss, and we might as well do it over lunch. Aunt Cora's housekeeper has provided me with a mountain of fish-paste sandwiches; she must think I need

50

feeding up. Do come up and join me!'

With one foot on the bottom stair, Maudie pulled the door shut behind her. Let the unlovely Bingo wait for his lunch. In any case, she wasn't about to discuss Mrs Groom's case in front of a layperson.

'This is what used to be the two bedrooms,' Lennox explained. 'I've had this one fitted out as a lounge-cum-dining area for ourselves, and through there is my office and storage area. I sleep and eat most of my meals up at the house, of course.'

'And the patients?' Maudie asked.

'I see them in what used to be the kitchen. There was water already laid on — useful for scrubbing up on occasion — and the back door means I can shoo them out that way instead of them tramping back through the waiting room. We didn't have to make too many changes, other than converting the old scullery into a lavatory. I couldn't bear to send sick people outside to the privy, even if that is all they have at home.'

'It all seems ideal, Dr Lennox. Now, I'm here because I have a bit of a problem.' She outlined Celia Groom's case, trying not to let her indignation show. It was not her place to complain to one doctor about another.

'Good old Don,' Dr Lennox said. 'He can be a bit abrupt at times, I know.' The two men had been medical school classmates and they were used to each other's foibles.

'I have advised Mrs Groom to seek a second opinion,' Maudie went on. 'Can I send her to you, or will that be construed as poaching on another doctor's preserve?'

'Oh, I don't think so, Nurse. Dean and I are in the same practice, of course, and if he's signed her off, so to speak, he can hardly complain.' Dr Dean's surgery was at Midvale, where he had taken over old Dr Mallory's house when that gentleman had retired and gone to live with his sister.

Removing the greaseproof paper from a plate of sandwiches, Dr Lennox told Maudie to help herself. 'You can come up now, Bingo old man!' he called down the stairs. Bingo appeared, looking resentful.

'Nurse, this is my cousin, Brian Munroe.'

'How do you do, Mr Munroe?'

'We've met,' he grunted. 'Oh, not fish-paste again! Why can't that wretched woman find egg or roast beef for a change? Perhaps Nurse can cater for us in future, if she's supposed to be part of this practice. She can take the money out of petty cash.'

'I'm a midwife, not a cook, Mr Munroe. I deliver babies, not lunches.'

The nerve of the man! Maudie eyed the plate of fast-disappearing sandwiches and reached out for another one. If Bingo disliked the filling so much, he wouldn't want one for himself, would he?

Dr Lennox laughed. 'We'll have to get you an apron, Bingo old chap. Then you can do a bit of cookery on the side. Perhaps you could manage some bangers and mash for a change.'

The look Bingo directed at his cousin would have stopped a charging bull at twenty paces, Maudie thought. There was a really venomous look in his eye. Now what on earth was all that about? Could the man not take a joke?

Later, cycling home in the teeth of a stiff wind, she thought what an ill-matched pair those two were. While the doctor seemed even-tempered and easy-going, Munroe appeared to have a chip on his shoulder. She could not detect any family resemblance, either. Maybe each man took after his own father, and that accounted for the difference.

She rather hoped that once the holiday season was over Bingo would be on his way, yet they were well into January and he seemed to be hanging on. She wondered if, having set up one nephew in practice here, Cora Beasley felt honour-bound to treat the other one in similar fashion. Not that he could set up in a medical practice, but the man must be capable of doing something.

Maudie hoped that whatever that might be, he would get on with it far away so she didn't have to put up with him much longer.

7

'Hello, Nurse! How nice to see you. We haven't seen each other since Christmas.' Mrs Blunt stood aside to let Maudie in. 'Beastly weather, isn't it? Neither one thing nor the other, though I'm sure I saw a few flakes of snow drifting down a while ago.'

Maudie shrugged off her gabardine coat, shaking it outside before turning back to hand it to her friend. 'I do hope it doesn't snow, though of course the children can't wait to see the white stuff! It makes it so difficult for me, trying to cycle through piles of slush.'

'Never mind. By next winter you'll be married and a housewife. No more rushing about in the cold and wet. Is that why you've come, to book a date for the wedding? I'm afraid Harold isn't here just now, but he should be back soon, if you care to wait. Do sit down, by the way. I'm forgetting my manners.'

'I don't know if there will be a wedding,' Maudie said.

Mrs Blunt stared at her. 'Don't tell me you two have had a falling out?'

Maudie shook her head. 'No, it's not that exactly.'

'You've been having second thoughts, then?'

'I suppose so, but it's not what you think. Dick has been offered the chance to go to Canada, to take part in some sort of rural policing thing. It's for six months, and he sails in April. He says he won't take it if I'm against it, but how can I ask him to give it up? It's the chance of a lifetime, Mrs Blunt.'

'Oh dear.'

'You see, taking part in this scheme may do his career some good, and at the same time he's thrilled with the idea of visiting places he never thought to see. You should just see him poring over the map, all eager and excited, like a big schoolboy. Some of the place names are so romantic: Moose Jaw, Medicine Hat, Eagle Falls.'

'So I suppose this means your wedding will have to be postponed until his return?

April May, June; he'll be back in the autumn, then. October is a lovely time for a wedding, I always think, with the Michaelmas daisies in bloom, and lovely bronze chrysanthemums. And of course there's always Christmas, with the church so beautifully decorated.'

Maudie sighed. 'You don't understand. He wants me to marry him as soon as possible, so I can go with him. We can honeymoon at Niagara Falls, he says.'

'Oh, how lovely! Well, I'm sure that Harold . . . '

'No!' Maudie cried. 'I've thought about this till I'm blue in the face, and I can't do it. But how am I going to break it to Dick? He'll be so hurt.'

Mrs Blunt leaned over and took Maudie's hand in hers. 'You feel he's rushing things, is that it? Or is it that you're not keen on marriage at all? You've been on your own for so long that you're bound to have become a bit set in your ways. Marriage will be a big adjustment, but then it always is. I do understand that.'

Maudie fiddled with the fringe of the

chenille tablecloth. 'I love Dick, and I do want to marry him. What I don't fancy is trotting along behind him like some sort of camp follower.'

Mrs Blunt laughed. 'Hardly that. You would be his wife.'

'Yes, but there's no provision for wives to go on this jaunt, or whatever you want to call it. I'll have to stay in digs, possibly all on my own, waiting for him to come looking for me in his spare time. I shan't know anybody, or how to go about doing the simplest things in a strange land. Even the money is different from our own.'

'It does sound a bit bleak.'

'You know, Mrs Blunt, twenty years ago I'd have jumped at a chance like this. Now I seem to have lost my sense of adventure.'

Mrs Blunt smiled gently. 'We were all young and reckless once, my dear, but life has a habit of sobering us up. It doesn't mean that there's anything lacking in our characters.'

'And there's another thing,' Maudie went on. 'I've just signed a contract for another year.'

'I hardly think that should stand in your way. Marriage is a good enough reason for leaving your job. I'm sure the Council will be delighted for you and they won't stand in your way at all.'

'But I'd be letting people down! And if I do stay on I'll be letting Dick down. I just don't know which way to jump.'

'May I make a suggestion, Nurse?'

'Of course. Go on.'

'Let's say you decide not to go to Canada. You could of course marry before Dick leaves. That way he'll know you love him and your decision to remain in England won't seem like such a personal rejection of him.'

'That's a thought.'

They were interrupted by the arrival of the vicar, which was Maudie's cue to get up and leave. Talking things over had been good for her, and she knew now what she meant to do.

* * *

While she was on the spot she decided to call in at her office in the parish hall. She hadn't been able to lay her hands on her fountain pen and she wondered if she might have left it there. She planned to spend the evening writing letters and besides, all the blotting paper she possessed was in the office. She would pick up a sheet to take home.

She had no sooner opened her desk drawer than a knock came at the door. She looked up to find a smartly dressed young woman standing in the doorway. Her style of dress proclaimed her to be a stranger to the area; none of the local women could afford garments like that. Unless Maudie was very much mistaken, the dress underneath the open coat was a Christian Dior original. The woman was tall and slender, and her blonde hair was professionally styled. It was difficult to say whether it was nature or an expensive hairdresser that had endowed her with that colour.

'Can I help you?'

'I want Dr Lennox. The woman at the post office told me he might be here.'

'I'm afraid not. Dr Lennox's surgery is a couple of miles down the road, in the gatehouse of the Beasley estate. Of course, he may not be there at this time of day. If this is a medical matter, perhaps I can advise you? I am a nurse.'

'This is personal.'

'I see.'

'If you'll be kind enough to give me directions I won't keep you any longer. I have my car so I should be able to track Lenny down.'

Lenny! That was a bit familiar, wasn't it? Who could this person be? Maudie longed to ask for details but good manners prevailed. 'I'll come outside with you and point you in the right direction, shall I? That will be easier than giving you verbal instructions when you don't know the district.'

When the woman had driven off in the smart little red roadster, Maudie mulled over what had just taken place, her own troubles momentarily forgotten. Could it be that Dr Lennox had a fiancée who had now come to claim him? The woman had worn gloves, making it impossible to see if she wore an engagement ring. Not that every future bride did; Maudie had yet to receive a ring from Dick.

Oh, he had certainly offered to buy one for her but she had refused, on the grounds that she wouldn't be able to wear it while in uniform. But this woman looked the type to insist on a diamond, the bigger the better.

It was odd that Mrs Hatch had sent the woman to Maudie's office. As postmistress she knew what was what in her district, and she was certainly aware of Dr Lennox's every move. She must have taken a dislike to their visitor, and once the local girls had caught a glimpse of the newcomer Mrs Hatch wouldn't be the only one. If it turned out that the doctor's fiancée had turned up out of the blue, that would really set the cat among the pigeons!

On the other hand, it might be all for the best if it stopped the silly girls from making fools of themselves, running around trying to get the poor man's attention. It was high time they regarded him as an efficient medical practitioner who was much more than just a handsome face.

The fountain pen wasn't there. Maudie slammed her desk door shut. She would have to go home and search the house again if she was to get those letters done tonight.

8

Dick listened quietly while Maudie tried to put her thoughts into words. 'And that's how it is,' she concluded. 'It would be different if you were a free agent and we could tour Canada together, but as things stand I just don't feel comfortable with the idea.'

'This is a chance that won't come again, Maudie. People like us can't afford to see the world, other than the odd day trip to Paris or something.'

'I know, and I'm sorry, but I know I can't do this. It's fear of the unknown, perhaps. Listen, Dick, this won't make any difference to us, will it? We'll still get married as planned, except that it will be an autumn or Christmas wedding instead of a traditional June one.'

Dick looked at her with his head on one side. 'I can't deny that I'm disappointed, Maudie, but I do understand. And of course it won't make any difference to us in the long run. Perhaps you might go along with part of my plan, though? It would make me so happy if you would.'

'What's that, then?'

'Let's get married before I leave. Then I'll know that you're back here waiting for me. Otherwise some other chap might snap you up while I'm away.'

'Don't be ridiculous! Where am I supposed to find another willing chap in Llandyfan?'

'That was a joke, old girl, but I'm quite serious about bringing the wedding forward. What's to stop us? We'll get married on a Saturday and perhaps we can get a few days off to have a little honeymoon somewhere. How about Yorkshire?'

'In the middle of winter? I've heard that the scenery up there is very beautiful, but it can be bleak at this time of year, just like anywhere else.'

'How about Bath, then? Or even London?'

'We'll see all those places in time, Dick,' Maudie told him gently, 'but I really can't agree to get married in such a rush. I saw too much of that happening during the war. You know, when men were about to be shipped off to fight, and they married their sweethearts so they could have one or two nights together before they left. I had to deliver the babies that resulted. Sometimes those men were killed before their children were born, and more often than not they never knew that their wives were expecting. My heart bled for those young mothers, left alone to bring up children who would never know their fathers.'

'Very distressing, I'm sure, but that's not likely to happen here, is it? For one thing I'm not off to the front, and neither am I going to the Wild West. I'll be back before you know it. And as for leaving you with a baby, you've already told me that you're too old to have children.'

'Thank you very much!'

'Sorry, Maudie. That didn't come out right. I'm just a bit disappointed, that's all, but I'll survive. You go ahead and make plans for an autumn wedding, and I'll fall in with whatever you decide. Agreed?'

Maudie nodded. When Dick had gone

she was left with the feeling that she'd been a bit of a bully. She'd shot down every one of his quite reasonable suggestions and come out the winner. She'd better watch herself, lest she turn into one of those women who wanted everything in a marriage done to her specifications. Not that she intended to live in subjugation to her husband, either. The marriage service might contain that nasty little bit about obedience, but there had to be some give and take as well.

★ ★ ★

As the weeks went by, Maudie was interested to see that the blonde stranger was staying on in the village. Her smart little red car could often be seen parked outside the Royal Oak, where she had taken a room. The local men could frequently be seen gathered around the little vehicle, patting it lovingly and discussing its merits.

Maudie suspected that the car's owner was just as much the subject of their conjecture as the vehicle itself. 'She's a smasher, is that one!' one fellow was heard to say, earning a glare from his wife. 'The car, love! I was talking about the car!' he mumbled, trying to redeem himself.

'Who is she?' Maudie asked, having run into the landlord's wife at the village shop. 'She called in to see me but she didn't give her name.'

'Paula Mason, her name is,' Dora Frost informed her.

'And what is she doing in Llandyfan?'

'She says she's engaged to marry Dr Lennox and she's come to visit him.'

'Sounds fishy to me,' Mrs Hatch said, as she neatly tipped the sugar she was weighing up into a blue paper bag. 'If she's his fiancée, why isn't she staying up at the big house? You tell me that! Cora Beasley is there to chaperone them, isn't she?'

'What does Miss Mason say about that, Mrs Frost?' Maudie asked.

Dora shrugged. 'She's pretty close-mouthed, Nurse. She clams up when we try to ask her anything and of course it's not our place to cross-examine our customers if they don't want to talk about themselves.

I did try to find out more, just by asking the sort of questions one woman does ask another. Will the wedding be here at St John's, that sort of thing. But she always changes the subject.'

'Nurse can find out for us,' Mrs Hatch said.

'What! How am I supposed to do that?'

'Ask Dr Lennox, of course. You're in pretty thick with him, aren't you? Just come out with it straight. Who is she? Where does she come from? Where does she get her money, seeing as she doesn't seem have a job at the moment?'

'Steady on, Mrs Hatch. For a start, I'm not 'in thick' with Dr Lennox, as you put it. We are professional colleagues and nothing more. It is certainly not my place to interrogate the man about his private life.'

'Not his, Nurse. Hers!'

'It's all part of the same thing.'

'Not necessarily. Listen, all you have to do is corner Dr Lennox and say something like, 'I hear that congratulations are in order.' Then when he smirks and says thank you, you go on to praise this Paula.

69

Lay it on a bit thick. Say how lovely she is, and how she dresses so smartly she puts us all to shame. Nothing wrong with that, is there?'

'I suppose I could try that,' Maudie said. 'But mind you, it will have to wait until I have some real reason for going up there. I can't just waltz in off the street and start probing for information. And come to think of it, is any of this really our business?'

'Our business? Of course it is. The doctor's wife will be part of the community, won't she? How are we supposed to rub along with her if she's some sort of mystery woman? For one thing, the doctor will probably get rid of that gloomy cousin of his and get his wife to run the surgery in his place. We all need to know what we have to deal with.'

'I hope he does,' Mrs Frost said. 'Get rid of that Mr Munroe, I mean. Awful man. I went up there last week and he demanded to know what I was there for. You know, Nurse, when I had the collywobbles and you told me what to do for it, but to get checked out after, just in

70

case. I mean, you don't want to tell that sort of thing to a strange man, do you? It's too personal.'

'That's true enough,' Mrs Hatch agreed. 'And what if anyone overheard? You don't want the whole world knowing your business, do you?'

Maudie struggled to keep a straight face. The postmistress didn't seem to realise that Paula Mason probably felt the same way. She might be a city girl, unused to the ways of country folk. What they saw as taking an interest, she most likely viewed as nosing in on things that did not concern them. She was entitled to her privacy, of course, but how maddening it was! The glamorous Miss Mason had been set down in their midst like a bird of paradise among a flock of little brown hens. Of course people were interested.

★ ★ ★

Maudie waited a week before going into action. The little red car remained parked outside the Royal Oak, and around the district tongues continued to wag. Maudie now had a legitimate reason for calling on Dr Lennox. She was just passing, she would say, and had come to enquire whether Mrs Groom had kept her appointment. She would arrive at lunchtime, not because she hoped to be offered more fish-paste sandwiches, but because the surgery was likely to be deserted at that time of day and she could catch the doctor by himself. She would get rid of the ever-present Bingo by mentioning doctor-patient confidentiality.

Propping her bicycle against the wall, she approached the gatehouse door, moving soundlessly in her crêpe-soled shoes. She stopped uncertainly at the sound of raised voices coming from inside.

' . . . turned me down flat!' That must be Bingo Munroe.

A female voice answered, dripping with scorn. 'Miserable little worm like you!' Maudie strained to hear more, but before she could gather her wits the door opened and a woman came flying out, almost colliding with her in the process.

Wasn't that Paula Mason? And why

was she on foot? The little red car was nowhere to be seen. Why had she come two miles on foot when she might have driven here in less than five minutes? Maudie shrugged and turned go inside, but before she could do so Bingo Munroe appeared in the doorway, his face red and his expression furious. He caught sight of Maudie and jumped back again, slamming the door. What on earth had been happening here?

9

'All right!' Maudie muttered. 'I can take a hint!' It wasn't urgent that she should see Dr Lennox when she had simply come here with an excuse. Having a word with Paula Mason would be much more productive. She turned to retrieve her bicycle, which had fallen down onto the frozen grass.

It wasn't long before she caught up with Miss Mason, who was marching along with her head down. 'Is there anything I can do to help?' she asked, dismounting from her machine and falling into step with her quarry.

'Help?' the woman said bitterly, without slackening her pace. 'Nobody can help me, unless you want to murder that wretched man!'

'Man? Do you mean Mr Munroe?'

'Bingo, and Lenny, and all creatures in trousers! They're all the same! You can't trust any of them. They're thoroughly useless. Don't you agree?'

'Oh, I do,' Maudie agreed, sending a silent apology to Dick, who was trustworthy, generous and kind, all rolled into one. 'Look, if you'd like to talk, I'm a good listener. It's part of my job as a nurse, to be there for people in distress.'

Paula looked at her for the first time. 'I suppose I could, but . . . '

'We'll go to the Copper Kettle,' Maudie said. 'We'll have a good old chinwag over a nice cup of coffee. How about it?'

When they were seated in the tearoom with cups of steaming coffee in front of them, Maudie eyed the three-tiered cake stand with interest. 'I think I'll have one of those éclairs,' she said. 'Blow the calories! I put in enough miles on my bike that I never put on an ounce.' That wasn't strictly true. She had recently been forced to let out her suspender belt by a couple of inches, but Paula couldn't know that. Maudie hoped to keep the woman here long enough to find out everything, and that might be accomplished if they both ordered food.

'What are you having?' she asked. 'That

chocolate cake looks scrumptious, or are you watching your figure?'

'What's the point?' Paula glared at the elderly waitress as if daring her to remonstrate. 'I'll have a piece of that, and an éclair as well. That'll show them!'

Just what she meant to show, and to whom, was a mystery to Maudie, but she sensed that she was about to find out. 'I couldn't help overhearing that you were having a bit of a disagreement with Mr Munroe,' she began. 'I've had words with him myself. He does tend to be overzealous when it come to looking after the doctor's well-being.'

'It wasn't a disagreement, as you call it.' Paula stirred her coffee more times than was necessary before slamming the spoon down on her saucer. 'He was trying to tell me that Lenny refuses to see me, that's what he was doing.'

'Surely not!'

'Oh, yes. I don't believe a word of it, of course. Bingo wants me for himself.'

'Really?'

Paula nodded. 'Oh, yes, and he'd say anything to get me away from Lenny. I'd bet any money that he's been telling lies to Lenny as well, just to help his cause along.'

'So you two knew each other before you came here, did you?'

'Of course we did. They are cousins, you know! A group of us used to go out together during the war and Bingo used to tag along with us when he come home on leave. He was always begging me to go out with him, looking at me with pleading eyes like a dog left out in the rain. Once he even asked me for a photo of myself, something he could pin up on the wall in the barracks like the other men did with snaps of their wives or sweethearts.'

'And did you let him have one?'

'Oh, no. You must know the type, Nurse! Give him an inch and he'd take a mile. I told him to get lost, of course.'

'Of course,' Maudie said. She could almost feel sorry for Bingo. It must be dreadful for him to be passed over for his luckier cousin. Bingo was weedy-looking and had no wealth or profession. Lennox was handsome and clever and had a position in society. It was no contest.

'Oh, well,' she murmured, 'I expect your fiancé will put Bingo in his place. Why don't you telephone him at the house, and let him know what's going on?'

'Don't think I haven't tried,' Paula said, mumbling through a mouthful of chocolate cake. 'They're all in it together, plotting against me. His Aunt Cora says he's in the bath and can't take the call. The housemaid says he's out, but she'll take a message. He must be there sometimes! I leave message after message, but he never calls me back. There's a perfectly good telephone at the Royal Oak but the landlord tells me there's never a call for me.'

'Then you'll just have to pop up there and wait to see him,' Maudie told her, knowing perfectly well that the girl had just tried that.

Paula glared at Maudie. 'What would you do if you were me?'

'I think I'd go home,' Maudie said, choosing her words with care. 'Men like to do the pursuing, don't they? They don't like it when girls show they're too interested. It's a leftover from the days when men were the mighty hunters and women cowered in caves, begging to be rescued from mammoths or something. That makes the men feel they're heroes, you see. We have to give them that impression, anyway,' she finished lamely. At least, that was the theory according to 'Ask Aunt Agatha' in the *Midvale Chronicle.*

'Heroes!' Paula spat, spilling cake crumbs all down her crêpe-de-chine blouse. 'I'll tell you what sort of hero your wonderful Dr Lennox is, shall I? He's strung me along for months, just using me, and now he says he doesn't want me anymore. He's broken off our engagement, you see, and that's why I'm here, to try to patch things up between us. It's just not fair, Nurse! I've done nothing wrong! It's that old aunt of his I blame. She doesn't think I'm good enough for her precious nephew!'

'I'm sorry to hear that, Miss Mason. This must be very hard for you, I'm sure. My advice still stands, however: I think you should put a brave face on things and quietly return home.'

'Well, Miss Clever-sticks Nurse, I don't think much of your advice! I mean to sue Leonard Lennox for breach of promise, and we'll see how he likes that!'

'Oh,' said Maudie, taken aback by Paula's vehemence, 'do you think you should? I mean, won't that let the whole world know that you've been, er . . . jilted?'

'And do you think I care about that?' Paula jumped to her feet and rushed out of the tearoom, leaving Maudie stuck with the bill for the pair of them. Maudie reached for the éclair that the girl had left behind. No point wasting good food, especially when she was paying for it!

'Fancy that!' The middle-aged waitress had come up behind Maudie without her noticing. 'Imagine her saying she's going to sue our nice young doctor for breach of promise. I didn't think people did that anymore, did you?'

'I don't know, Mary. You used to see that all the time in the *News of the World* years ago, but I think the war put paid to that sort of business. People had better things to think about than getting money out of faithless lovers.'

'Do you think she'll do it, then?'

'I think she'll live to rue the day if she does. It may give her some satisfaction for a while, but would you want the whole world knowing you'd been ditched, Mary? Better to go away and lick one's wound in private, I should have thought.'

'Ah, that's because it's never happened to you, Nurse. But what if that Constable Bryant of yours decided to call off your wedding? Would you go quietly then?'

'I hope I'd manage to act with dignity,' Maudie said. 'How about you, Mary? Would you make a big public fuss, just to make a show of the chap?'

'I never had the chance to find out what I might do, Nurse. My old mum was an invalid for years and I was the only one able to take care of her. I never went to dances or night school, and the only men I ever saw were the milkman and the postman, and both of them were married. By the time Mum passed away, God rest her soul, I was past caring. I'd lost my looks and now I have to work all hours here to support myself. Who would look at me, Nurse?'

81

Maudie sighed. 'It's a hard life, right enough. All we can do is to keep putting one foot in front of the other and moving on, like that Harry Lauder song. 'Keep right on to the end of the road.' Is that my bill you have there, Mary? I'd better be getting home. By the look of that sky we're in for some weather.'

10

A pounding on the front door brought Maudie to her feet. She'd been sitting at the kitchen table, still in her petticoat, about to indulge in a second cup of tea. What now? It could not be the arrival of a desperate husband come to announce the imminent birth of a baby, because nobody was due for weeks. Snatching up a sheet that had been drying on the clothes-horse, she wrapped it around herself sari-fashion.

The woman on the doorstep was past middle age, with a red face contorted in pain. Her grey hair was all over the place, as if she had left home in a hurry without stopping to put it up in a turban. Maudie noticed that the woman's left hand was wrapped in a tea towel from which water was dripping.

'Come in! Come in! Have you had an accident?'

'I put me hand through the wringer. You're a nurse, aren't you? That woman in the shop pointed you out to me the other day. 'That's Nurse Rouse, that is,' she said. 'Go to her if you're ever in trouble, she'll set you right.' So here I am.'

'That's all very well,' Maudie said, unwrapping the cloth and surveying the swollen hand. 'You should have called for an ambulance and gone to casualty right away. Never mind that now; let's see what we can do for you. I wish I had some ice, but we'll have to make do with a basin of cold water. Just sit there at the table while I get one, and then I expect you could do with a cup of tea. There's plenty in the pot. And you'd better take a couple of Aspro while we're at it. You'll be in pain soon, if you're not already. I must say, I'm surprised your hand isn't worse, if it went through the mangle.'

'Oh, my daughter was there, and she come running when I yelped. Stopped the beastly thing before it could suck my whole arm in.'

When the patient had been made as comfortable as possible under the circumstances, Maudie told her that, like it or not, she would have to go to the hospital in case any of the bones in her hand had been broken. 'It's all free now, you know. It won't cost you a penny, if that's what's worrying you.'

'I know all that, Nurse. It's just that I don't trust those places. My great aunt Alice, she went in with a busted hip and she never came out again — at least, not alive. Got that there new moany thing, she did.'

'I'm afraid that often happens to elderly people when they've been immobilised by a serious fracture,' Maudie explained. 'Coming down with pneumonia, that is. I suspect that she was much older than you, though; am I right? And awkward though this may be for you, it won't stop you walking about. It's being immobile that causes the trouble.'

When the woman had reluctantly given way, Maudie phoned the ambulance station and was told that the patient would be collected shortly. She retuned to the table. 'Now then, can I get your name and address for my records? I'm Maudie Rouse, by the way.'

'Hilda Beckett, twelve Cherry Way.'

'Cherry Way? I don't think I . . . '

'It's the new prefabs, Nurse.'

'Oh, yes? And very nice, too.'

'That's what I thought until last night.'

'Oh, what happened then?'

'Some idiot chucked half a brick through next door's front window. Made a right old mess on her good carpet, too. She says she'll never be able to get all the bits of glass out, and her with kiddies in the house.'

'Toddlers, are they?'

'No, eleven-year-old twins. Holly and Hazel. Pretty names, aren't they?'

'Have they called the police? Do they know who threw the brick? Local yobs, perhaps?'

'Mrs Neville — that's my neighbour — she thinks it must be somebody from the village, on account of the note that was wrapped around it and tied on with a bit of string. 'Go back where you come from, it said. 'We don't want no foreigners here.' Not spelled right, neither.'

'Oh, dear.'

'Mind you, I don't know what they

mean about foreigners. We're all English, except for the chap at the end of the street. Dai Morris, his name is. Welsh.'

'I think that anyone whose grand-parents weren't born in the parish are thought of as foreigners,' Maudie said, laughing. 'They probably call me one, behind my back! I shouldn't worry about it. It was probably someone who'd had one too many in the Royal Oak.'

'That's as may be. What I want to know is, who is going to pay for new window glass? And what if happens again? Living through the war was bad enough. I thought this was supposed to be peacetime. I feel all of a dither, and now look what's hap-pened!'

'Don't you worry, Mrs Beckett. The police will get to the bottom of it. Now then, how is that hand of yours? Have the Aspro done anything to deaden the pain?'

'It hurts like the dickens, Nurse, but I daresay I'll have to put up with it, and me with my washing only half done!'

'They'll look after you well at the cottage hospital,' Maudie promised.

Later that day Maudie dropped in at

the shop to buy a Reckett's blue bag. Her white sheets and towels had taken on a distinctly greyish look and bluing them would help restore them. They hadn't had enough sun recently to bleach whatever was put out on the line.

Mrs Hatch greeted her with a loud cry. 'There you are, Nurse! I saw the ambulance at your door and I thought something had happened to you. Fallen down the stairs, p'raps!'

'After overdoing it at the Royal Oak, you mean,' Maudie said with a straight face. Mrs Hatch frowned.

'Overdoing it at . . . oh, you're making a joke, are you?'

Maudie rolled her eyes. 'The ambulance was for a patient. Someone I had to send to hospital for treatment.'

'Well, now! Who was taken poorly, then?'

'You know I can't discuss cases, Mrs Hatch.'

The postmistress pouted. 'I don't see why not. It'll be all over the village by teatime anyway. And have you heard about the trouble at the prefabs?'

'Yes I have, as a matter of fact, and it's

disgusting. That's no way to welcome newcomers to the village. And where are they going to find the glass to put in a new window? Like everything else, it's still in short supply.'

'It'll be youths, I expect. Not from round here, of course. Children are brought up properly in this neighbourhood. It'll be strangers coming in on those noisy motorbikes they have. You set your Dick Bryant on them, Nurse. We'll soon have them sent to borstal, where they'll get the birching they deserve. That'll teach them a lesson.'

Mrs Hatch looked quite fierce. Typical, thought Maudie. When murder or mayhem occurs, it's never done by one of your own. It must be strangers from beyond the pale.

Suddenly she recalled what Fred Miller had said. He had insisted that there was bound to be trouble between the villagers and the incomers. Surely he hadn't heaved a brick through the Nevilles' window? He could be a bit awkward at times, but he was a grandfather. Would he do such a thing at a house where there were children who might get hit with flying glass? Besides, how would he make his way up to where the prefabs were? He never ventured far from home, being a bit shaky on his pins. And his daughter Daisy kept a sharp eye on him. No, it could have nothing to do with Fred.

What about his cronies, though? They might at least know something. Maudie made up her mind to go and see Dora Frost, the wife of the landlord at the Royal Oak. She might have overheard something. Throughout history men seemed to have got together in pubs to plan their nefarious actions, so why should anything be different now?

And while she was there she would think up some excuse to go and see Paula Mason, who was staying upstairs. Not that it was any of her business really, she reminded herself yet again, but she was intrigued by the situation. Maudie couldn't really imagine any woman in her right mind starting a breach of promise action. Why expose yourself to the world as a jilted woman? Surely it was much better to creep away to lick your wounds in private, even if it did mean letting the man in question get off scot-free.

This was very much the stuff of the Victorian age. If a woman was betrayed by a man and left with a baby and no means of support, she might well try to get him to face up to his responsibilities, but this was 1949. Nowadays, Maudie supposed, the thing to do was to hire a solicitor and get him to apply for a maintenance order. But as far as she knew Paula Mason wasn't pregnant, and she certainly hadn't said anything about being a mother already.

Maudie hoped for Dr Lennox's sake that all this talk of court action was so much hot air. This sort of thing could ruin the career of any professional man, let alone a doctor.

11

Maudie was in her office, taking stock of the supplies of items needed for making up maternity packs. These were taken to the homes of patients well in advance of their delivery dates, so that everything was in place when the great day arrived,

'Or night, probably,' she reminded herself. It was amazing, really, how many babies decided to enter the world in the small hours, and she was well accustomed to being roused from sleep by some anxious father or neighbour, summoning her to action.

An unearthly squeal alerted her that somebody had opened the door of the parish hall. Really, that Pratt wanted shooting! How many time had she requested he give the hinges a drop of oil? She supposed she'd have to do it herself if the sexton couldn't, or wouldn't, get a move on.

'Hello, Nurse! Have you got a minute?'

'Dr Lennox! Yes, of course. Come right in and take a pew.' She waved a hand in the direction of the comfortable chair that was kept for patients and visitors. 'What can I do for you?'

'Do you mind if I close this door?' he asked. 'I have no wish to be overheard.'

Maudie nodded. She usually left it open because her office space was so very small. It could get quite claustrophobic in here with the door closed. She had a sickening feeling that she was about to get a rocket. Had Miss Mason complained to him that Maudie had been meddling in her business?

The doctor sat down carefully, pulling on the legs of his trousers to prevent them from creasing. He cleared his throat. 'Nurse Rouse. Maudie. You're a woman, aren't you?'

She raised her eyebrows. 'I was indeed, the last time I looked.'

'Then you must know what make women tick. Probably.'

The man was obviously struggling and she decided to help him out. 'Do you have a difficult female patient, Dr Lennox? Is that it?'

'Not a *patient*, Nurse,' he said, scratching his forehead.

So that was it! Miss Mason was giving him a hard time. A little voice in her head told Maudie that she should nip this in the bud before he had a chance to say something they'd both regret later. She really mustn't get involved in whatever was happening between these two people. Jumping in with both feet could lead to trouble.

She ignored the little voice. The man had come all the way here looking for help, so why not give it? If it satisfied her own vulgar curiosity at the same time, so what?

'Are you sure you want to tell me this?' she began. 'I gather this is a personal matter, and I'm not quite sure why you've come to me.'

'I have to get something off my chest, Nurse, and I've nobody else to confide in. You're a professional colleague and I know that ethics will prevent you from blabbing all over the place. Am I right?'

'Of course.' Maudie felt flattered that a doctor would confide in her, but then where else could he turn? Dr Dean was unlikely to give him any sympathy, and Cousin Bingo was a lost cause. 'What seems to be troubling you, Dr Lennox?'

'It's Paula Mason. I take it you've met her, Nurse?'

'Your fiancée? Oh yes, of course.'

'She's not my fiancée!' he snapped.

'I see.'

'No, Nurse, I don't think you do. The wretched woman is putting it about that I've jilted her, when I've done no such thing. I have never asked her to marry me. We have never been engaged. I can't imagine why she is saying these things!'

'But you did know each other before she came to Llandyfan looking for you?'

'Oh, yes. When I was a medical student a gang of us used to go round together in our meagre off-duty time. Nothing special, you know; just the odd country hike or going to watch a rugger game. We all used to pair off occasionally and I took Paula to the pictures once or twice. There was nothing in it and I suppose we drifted apart, the way you do when you're young.'

'And that was all?' Maudie asked. 'You

haven't seen the woman since?'

'Well, she did turn up at my graduation — uninvited, I might add. And she tended to pop up from time to time at friends' parties, that sort of thing. But no, I haven't been seeing her in that sense of the word.'

'So the upshot is she's stalking you?'

'You could put it like that, but why? What does she hope to gain by it? She must be mad.'

'Perhaps she fancies herself as a doctor's wife,' Maudie murmured. 'And forgive me for saying so, Dr Lennox, but you are very nicely placed here, aren't you? You've been set up in practice by a wealthy, childless aunt who may very well leave you her money when he dies.'

Lennox stared at her. 'My, my, the gossips have been busy, haven't they!'

Maudie shrugged. 'You did ask for my opinion, Dr Lennox. And if what you say is true, then Miss Mason is either mentally ill or totally misguided.'

'It beggars belief!' he said, leaning back in his chair. 'She couldn't hope to blackmail me into marriage.'

'Of course,' Maudie said slowly, 'there could be some other explanation.'

'Such as?'

'She may be upset with you for some totally different reason, and this is her way of making you pay.'

'That's nonsense.'

'Then could it have something to do with your family? I overheard her having words with Mr Munroe the other day and their argument seemed quite heated.' Maudie didn't offer an explanation as to how and where she had heard this, and she hoped he wouldn't ask.

'Poor old Bingo! So loyal. I expect he was only trying to protect me from the stupid woman. And if anyone has occasion to feel upset in this situation, it's poor old Bingo.'

'Oh?'

'Yes indeed. He was very much taken with Paula at one time, but she made it clear that she wasn't interested.'

'So they knew each other before, then.'

'Oh, yes. My mother always felt protective of her sister, Bingo's mother. I think she felt guilty that she was fairly well off as the wife of a successful doctor, when Aunt Mona had to struggle to make ends meet. So Mother used to invite them to come to us for Christmas, and to join us on seaside holidays, that sort of thing. Bingo happened to be staying with us once when Paula was part of our gang, just a group of young people who played tennis together and so on.'

'And Mr Munroe met Paula and fell in love, I suppose.'

'She, of course, couldn't have cared less, which meant that he went around with a face like a wet week in Brighton, which didn't impress her one bit. He is much older than Paula, which didn't help. She was just at that stage where having men fall at her feet, so to speak, was a bit of a hoot to her. She didn't care whose feelings she trampled on.'

'The way you tell it, she doesn't seem like a very nice person,' Maudie murmured, fascinated by this unexpected glimpse into the doctor's family life.

'It all came to a head when Bingo was called up to join the army. He asked Paula if he might have a snap of her, to display above his bed in the barracks. You know the sort of thing, Nurse — photos of wives, pin-up posters and all the rest.'

Never having entered an army barracks, Maudie didn't know, but she nodded eagerly, willing him to continue.

'It wouldn't have done her any harm to give the man a snap of herself. In fact I should have thought she have been flattered to be asked. But no! She tore him off a strip in front of all of us, calling him a miserable little worm that no sane woman would look at twice. Poor old Bingo; he doesn't have much to recommend him, but he didn't deserve that. Now the wretched woman is hanging round my neck, and I don't know what to do about her. That's why I've come to you. You must know how women think. How they react in given situations.'

'I'm afraid I can't see inside the mind of a woman like her,' Maudie assured him. 'She sounds to me like a thoroughly nasty piece of work. I was brought up to be careful of other people's feelings, and if I had to give some chap the brush-off I'd do it as kindly as possible, unless he was being obnoxious. I certainly can't identify with your Miss Mason. I'll give you my opinion, for what it's worth, though I can't promise that it will work. I suggest you sit down with the woman and let her know, gently but firmly, that you are not interested in marrying her. If she gives you an argument, let her know that you intend to consult a solicitor about taking out some kind of restraining order. Then make an appointment with him, and follow through.'

12

'I've had a brilliant idea!' Dick told Maudie. They were sitting in the Copper Kettle, sipping coffee and sharing a large slice of Battenberg cake.

Maudie licked her lips appreciatively. 'That was delicious. Ordering only one slice was a mistake. Shall we have another one?'

'I don't mind if I do. Did you hear what I said, Maudie?'

'You've had an idea.'

'Yes. I thought you weren't paying attention. Well, you know I sail for Canada on the fourteenth of April?'

'Yes, you've mentioned it often enough.' Maudie didn't want to think about it. The idea of being without Dick for six months was beginning to hit home, and she was sorry now that she'd refused to go to Canada with him.

'Well, why don't you come to Liverpool to see me off?'

'What? I can't do that!'

'Of course you can. We'll go up on the train and stay in a B & B overnight. Then you can come on board and have a look round. When I write to you from the ship you'll be able to see it all in your mind's eye. How about it, then?'

'I suppose I could, if I could get the time off.'

'Of course you can. You must have holidays due to you.'

Indeed she did. She had been saving them up so she could go on honeymoon with her new husband, but that wasn't going to happen now, or at least not for some time to come.

'Yes, I'll do it!' she said, in her excitement bringing her fist down on the table with a bang. To her great dismay and embarrassment she found herself clutching the handle of her coffee cup and not much else; the main part of the cup lay smashed on the tablecloth.

'There's been an accident!' Dick declared, trying to hide a grin and not succeeding.

'I'm so sorry, Mary. It came apart in

my hand!' Red-faced, Maudie bit her lip as the waitress came hurrying over.' I'll pay for it, of course. And for that to be laundered,' she added, as an ominous brown stain appeared on the tablecloth.

'Lucky you didn't cut yourself, Nurse, or where would we all be then? You couldn't deliver babies with a whopping great bandage on your hand. It wouldn't be hygienic at all. And never you mind about that there cup. That fool girl who comes in to wash up is always smashing things. I'll just slip this one in with the other breakages.'

'She won't have to pay for it, will she?'

'No, no. The lady who owns this place has been threatening to dock the girl's wages if she don't smarten up, but it's never happened yet. I'll just fetch you another cup of coffee, shall I?'

'I don't think so, thanks, but we would like another slice of that delicious cake, please.'

'You better leave her a decent tip,' Dick whispered when the waitress had departed. 'Now, what were you saying before the ceiling crashed down on our ears?'

'I said I'll come to see you off at Liverpool. And I'd love to see round the ship, just so long as this isn't some ploy of yours to whisk me off to Canada. You needn't think you can lock me in a cabin until the ship sails!'

'I'd never aid and abet a stowaway,' Dick told her, laughing. 'Anyway, you don't have a passport, do you, so they won't let you into Canada.'

'Have they told you which ship you'll be sailing on?'

'Yes. The *Empress of France*. It's one of the steamships of the Canadian Pacific line. It used to be the *Duchess of Bedford,* a cargo and passenger boat that was converted to a troop ship during the war.'

Maudie wrinkled her nose. 'I don't like the idea of you going all that way on some old tub. I was just a toddler when the *Titanic* went down, but I can still remember all the grown-ups talking about the tragedy. It was supposed to be unsinkable, but look what happened!'

Dick laughed. 'The *Empress* was refitted two years ago. It's a luxury liner now. Mind you, I'll be going tourist class, but that doesn't mean they'll have us all battened down in the hold. I understand I'll be in a two-berth cabin with another fellow, which shouldn't be too bad.'

Maudie licked her forefinger and applied it to the crumbs on her plate. Dick raised his eyebrows. She raised hers in return. 'Waste not, want not,' she informed him.

Angry shouts were heard from outside. Mary crossed to the window and looked out. 'There's two men chasing a boy,' she announced. 'I suppose the little devil's been up to mischief. You never know what kiddies will get up to nowadays. I blame it on the war, that's what.' She flung the door open. 'If you want the coppers, there's one in here!' she bawled.

Dick sighed. 'Bang goes my evening off! Well, I suppose I'd better see what's going on.'

Two men appeared in the doorway, one of them holding a struggling child by the ear.

'Careful!' Maudie admonished. 'You'll have his ear off! And what have you been up to now, Johnny Grayson?'

'You know this boy, Nurse?' The larger of the two men tipped his cap to Maudie.

Yes, she knew the child. She had treated him for nits at the school, persuaded him to get vaccinated against diphtheria, and brought his little brother into the world. He was a little scamp, but his crimes were no worse than those perpetrated by others of his age group. Scrumping apples, or putting a toad in the teacher's desk, were about his limit.

'Sit down, both of you,' Dick ordered. 'Not you, boy. Stay where you are, and stand up straight. Now then, what's been happening?'

'I was over at the prefabs, delivering coal,' the shorter man said. Maudie had already noticed his grubby suit and dirty hands that made it appear as if he had come straight from a coal mine. 'I was about to drive off when I saw this boy here with half a brick in his hand. I hollered at him just as he let fly with it and it missed the window he seemed to be aiming at and hit the wall instead.' He turned to the boy. 'You needn't bother applying to play on the Llandyfan cricket

106

team, boy. You'll never make a decent bowler, and that's a promise!'

The child shuffled his feet, saying nothing.

'And what happened then?' Dick prompted.

'I had to get on with my rounds, and the boy ran off, so I just kept going. But when I got to the Royal Oak I saw him again, skulking round outside. That's when I stopped to ask him what he was playing at; only he took off again, with me in pursuit. And Dobbins here, he joined me.'

'How did you know it was the same boy?' Maudie wondered.

'Take a look at his pullover, miss. You won't find two of them in a month of Sundays.'

True enough, she thought. In true make-do-and-mend fashion, someone had used up scraps of wool to knit what was undoubtedly a warm garment, although garish in colour. Red, blue, navy and green were splashed at random across the front of the jersey, like a rainbow gone mad.

'What were you doing at the pub?' Dick

demanded. 'Planning to throw another brick, were you?'

'I was waiting for my dad,' the child said.

'Bill Grayson,' Maudie said, out of the side of her mouth. 'The Royal Oak is his second home.'

'I see. And what about your mum, boy? Where is she?'

'She works up the button factory over Midvale, mister.'

'Sir. You can call me sir,' Dick said.

'Yes, sir.'

'Now then, why were you throwing a brick at that house? Did you have a grudge against someone who lives there?' No answer. Dick turned to his audience, who were following the exchange avidly. 'When this happened the first time we suspected old Josiah Jones, the chap who likes to spend Christmas being detained at His Majesty's pleasure. However, it's not like him to do anything amiss at this time of year, when it's warm enough to sleep out of doors. So we've been looking for someone with a motive to cause trouble at the prefabs, and we seem to have caught our man!'

'And if he was my lad he'd get a good thrashing!' Dobbins declared.

Seeing the child's frightened look, Dick smiled at him kindly.

'Will I go to prison, mister?'

'No, no, boy. But if you carry on like this, mind, you could end up in borstal one of these days. And you wouldn't like that!' The dreaded institution for young offenders did not take in children of this boy's age, but the child had no way of knowing that.

'So why did you do it, Johnny?' Maudie asked him.

The boy rubbed his eyes with a grimy paw. 'I did it to help Mum,' he whispered.

13

Maudie was surprised when Rita Grayson turned up to see her the following morning. Throwing herself into the visitor's chair, the woman began her complaint without preamble.

'I think I'm in the family way, Nurse. Again! At my age! Why me? That what I want to know.'

Maudie could have said that any married woman was likely to find herself in a similar state, but she bit her tongue. The woman was obviously in distress and with four boys at home, including a two-year-old, her misgivings were easily understood.

'I don't know how much more I can stand, Nurse! That man of mine is no use to man or beast, spending all his dole down the Royal Oak. And me working all hours in the button factory for next to nothing. And the boys eat us out of house and home, never mind I have to pay

Mum something for taking the baby during the day. If I have to stop work I just don't know how we'll manage. And to cap it all, I've had the police round. Young Johnny's been in trouble, and him just turned eleven.'

Maudie could see that the woman was on the verge of tears, so first things first. Having listened to a recital of the woman's symptoms, she asked her to climb up onto the examination couch.

'I can't tell definitely without the usual test,' she said at last, 'but I don't think you are expecting, Mrs Grayson.'

'But I've not had the curse for two months! And I'm always tired like this when I'm expecting. When you've had four kiddies you get to know the signs.'

'Anyone would be exhausted with the workload you're carrying, Mrs Grayson. And as for the other business — let's see, how old are you now?'

'Forth-five come August.'

'Yes, well, my guess is you're approaching the menopause.'

'Aw, no, not that! Haven't I enough to put up with without going doolally as well?'

Maudie laughed. 'That's old-fashioned thinking, Mrs Grayson. It's true that a woman's hormones may be all over the place then, but that doesn't mean that we all go off our heads! Personally I'm looking forward to it. I'll be glad to be done with all that monthly business.'

'But why am I so tired all the time?'

'Let's see, now. You get up early, catch a bus to Midvale, put in a day's work and then do the journey in reverse. When you get home you have your hubby and boys to see to, meals to cook, housework to catch up on. You never have a minute to yourself, do you? And when did you last go to the pictures, or have a day out at the seaside?'

'Hmph!'

'Now then. Your periods will probably come back, although they may not be regular. You must try to pay attention to your diet and, hard as it may be, you must try to get some rest. Encourage your hubby to do a bit now and then.'

'Huh! You might as well ask the birds to come down out of the trees and tackle the washing-up. Bill Grayson wasn't made to do women's work, Nurse.'

'Surely he can help with the boys, Mrs Grayson. Take them out to play football or something. Outside of school hours they need something to keep them out of mischief.'

'You heard about our Johnny's trouble, then?'

The sadness in the woman's eyes was so apparent that Maudie felt a pang of sympathy, but she pressed on. 'I happened to be with Constable Bryant when your little boy was brought in.'

'How could he do such a thing?' Mrs Grayson blurted. 'He's been taught right from wrong; they all have. We're respectable people, Nurse. Oh, I know people say my Bill takes a drop more than he should, but that's only on account of him not being able to find work. It makes him feel a failure, see. But he'd never do what that boy did. I don't know how to stop that child from going to the bad, Nurse. Throwing bricks through other people's windows — I never heard the like!'

'I heard Johnny say that he did it to help you,' Maudie murmured.

Mrs Grayson's jaw dropped. 'What? Dick Bryant never told me that! Are you sure? Why would the little devil come out with a thing like that? Oh, when I get hold of him I'll tan his britches for him good and proper, you see if I don't!'

'Are you sure he hasn't overheard you saying something against the Nevilles, Mrs Grayson? Something that led him to believe they should be punished for something, let's say?'

'Why, no. Dot Neville and I work at the same place. We sit together on the bus of a morning. She's all right, is Dot, although she does go on a bit about those girls of hers and how clever they are at the school. Oh!' A tide of red colour surged across the woman's face and neck. Maudie waited. For a long moment only the ticking of the clock on the wall broke the silence.

'Is there something you'd like to tell me, Mrs Grayson?' Maudie prompted at last.

'Oh, Nurse, what have I done? I never meant things to come to this!' She broke down and began to sob.

'And that's what it was all about,' Maudie told Dick when they went walking that evening. 'Young Johnny is about to sit the eleven plus, as they call it.'

'And he's nervous about it, is that it? No reason to go mad with a brick in his hand, though, is it?'

The eleven plus examination was the result of the Education Act of 1944. Its purpose was to determine the type of secondary education that each child would receive, whether at a grammar school, a secondary modern or a technical school. There was fierce competition among parents to get their children into a grammar school which, they hoped, was the first step towards a good career. Those with the right qualifications might even go on to attend university, which was a grand dream among parents who had not received much education themselves.

'Mrs Grayson is desperate to get Johnny into Midvale Grammar,' Maudie explained. 'Her family is having such a hard time, and she's pinned her hopes on Johnny being able to better his chances. Going to that school is the first step.'

'And?'

'So she's afraid that something will get in the way of that. The two little Neville girls are very bright, apparently. Their mother is always boasting to Rita Grayson about how clever they are, and how they are certain to get into the grammar school. The thing is, there are only so many scholarships available, and now these two have moved into the area the competition is that much tougher.'

'That's ridiculous. There must be hordes of kiddies getting ready to sit the exam. Brookfield and Midvale are teeming with youngsters. Those twins could get pipped at the post.'

'True, but all Rita can see is that her Johnny has to get into that school if he's to have the sort of future she envisions for him. Well, according to her, she was having a moan to her mum, saying that if only those twins hadn't come to Llandyfan the boy might have had a fighting chance. Somebody ought to heave a brick through their window, let them know they're not wanted here. Then perhaps they'd go back where they came from.'

'And the boy overheard and thought he'd better give her a hand,' Dick grunted. 'And when it didn't work the first time he thought he'd try it again, and that's when he was caught.'

'As Mrs Grayson explained to me, she didn't mean it, of course. It's just one of those silly things you say in the heat of the moment, like saying, 'My dad will kill me if I don't get home by ten o'clock.' Now she's terrified that even if the boy does win a scholarship he won't be able to take it up because he has a criminal record.'

'Hardly that, old girl. He's been given a good talking-to, and his father has threatened to give him a good lambasting if he ever tries anything like that again, so that should see the end of it. Mind you, replacing that window glass is going to cut into Bill Grayson's boozing money, so I'd say the little rascal should keep his distance for the moment if he wants to avoid that threat coming true.'

Maudie sometimes regretted not having married earlier and having children of her own, but when she saw the difficulties that some parents went through she couldn't help feeing glad that she was single. Now, though, she wondered if she had been wise. Looking at Dick, she thought it might be have been rather pleasant to have a little boy resembling him, although of course that wouldn't have been the case if she had married someone else! It was a good thing she hadn't done that, for Dick was worth waiting for. She smiled.

'What's up, old girl?'

She grinned at Dick. 'Oh, nothing. Only thinking.'

He took her hand and squeezed it. 'You really worry about your patients and their families, don't you?'

'I'm supposed to maintain some professional detachment, but yes, of course I care. And that means that I have to do what I can to help, above and beyond delivering babies. What is life all about if we can't reach out to help others?'

14

Maudie called in to see Mrs Blunt. 'I've come to let you know that I'll be away next week. I'm taking three days off.'

'That's nice, Nurse. At least, I hope it is. I don't mean to pry, but you're not going into hospital or tests or anything, are you?'

'No, no. Nothing like that. Just a bit of a break, really. Anyway, I'll post a notice on the door of the office telling people to contact Dr Lennox is anything untoward happens, although luckily I have nobody close to term at the moment. I thought you should know in case someone turns up here in a panic.'

There was no police station at Llandy-fan, and prior to the coming of Dr Lennox people had turned to Maudie in an emergency, and failing that, to the vicar. Even now, some patients had not fully grasped the idea that medical attention could be obtained free of charge, and they hesitated to turn up at the surgery. In addition to that, most of the women — the older ones especially — preferred to discuss their ailments with another woman.

'Going somewhere nice?' Mrs Blunt asked, trying not to sound inquisitive and failing.

Maudie smiled at her friend. 'Liverpool.'

'Liverpool! Do you have friends up there you're going to see?'

'No, I don't know anyone there.'

'Then why on earth? I'm sure Liverpool is a very nice place to visit, but what I mean is, it's so far away. If you're only taking three days, two of them will be taken up with travelling, what with changing trains and all. You'll only have one full day to see the sights.'

Maudie took pity on her. 'I'm going there to see Dick off to Canada. He sails on the *Empress of France* on Thursday.'

'Oh! Oh, I see. And where will you — er . . . ' Her voice tapered off.

'We'll be staying in a B & B, Mrs Blunt. Two separate B & Bs.'

'Oh, yes, of course.'

'We'll have the time together travelling

up, and the next day I'll be able to go on board with him and have a good look round the ship. Then I'll be able to visualise what he's doing while he's crossing the Atlantic.'

'I see. You're not having second thoughts now, are you? Perhaps wishing you were going with him after all?'

'It's too late now if I did,' Maudie assured her. 'I wouldn't be able to get a passport in time. Anyway, he's only going for six months. The time will go by in a flash.'

'Of course it will.' The vicar's wife had spent all her married life consoling people in trouble and trying to get anxious parishioners to look on the bright side. Now she felt herself to be on shaky ground. Practical, capable Nurse Rouse always seemed to be in charge, no matter what the situation, but this was new territory for her. Joan Blunt wondered what would happen if Dick Bryant took a shine to Canada and decided to stay. Could that spell the end of their relationship? She sincerely hoped not. Maudie deserved her bit of happiness.

Maudie made a list. Dick had counselled her to travel light. 'We'll be going about on foot when we get to Liverpool,' he said. 'We don't want to be lugging blooming great suitcases around, and this way we can do without porters, too. It's not that I'm tight-fisted, you know, but tips add up and I expect I'll need to save my money for the ship. We're expected to give a percentage of the fare to our cabin steward, and I'm sure there will be other expenses as well.'

It was all very well for Dick to talk about travelling light; his trunk has been send ahead to the ship, and would be waiting for him when he went on board. Besides, men could manage on just a few things; perhaps a change of shirt, socks and underwear and they were all set. It was different for women.

Nightclothes. She had to pack her heavy dressing gown because she didn't want to be seen in her flimsy nightgown while flitting back and forth to the bathroom. What if there were male guests in the house, or the landlady's husband or sons? If only she had a glamorous negligee! But it wasn't worth the expense of buying one at this stage. Time enough for that when she went on honeymoon with Dick.

Undies. Stockings. Her wash bag, with everything that entailed. A spare skirt, and the court shoes that matched it. She couldn't wear the brown shoes she meant to travel in when she switched to her navy blue skirt. A cardigan, of course, in case the weather turned cold. And what about a blouse? She had two that went well with the navy skirt. The one with a design of small poppies was her favourite, but the collar was starting to fray and there was no time to turn it. The cut of the striped one was too boxy and made her look fat. Which should she choose? Decisions, decisions!

Having assembled everything to her satisfaction, she stuffed it all into a canvas grip, wishing she had one of those rucksacks beloved of hikers. At least the grip would be easier to manhandle than her enormous cardboard suitcase. She would leave that gathering dust on top of her wardrobe.

Now for the contents of her handbag,

she thought. A stick of barley sugar to eat on the train, to ward off possible travel sickness. Comb, mirror, lipstick, powder compact. Money, pen, notebook, a cellophane strip containing Aspro tablets, a clean handkerchief. Better make that two hankies, in case one was needed if she had to administer first aid to someone.

She would make sandwiches first thing in the morning, to add to the cake she had already made. Those could travel in her faithful string shopping bag. 'We'll have a meal on the train,' Dick had promised, and indeed, eating in the dining car would be a treat. But the local train, which they had to take first, was unlikely to be a corridor train, and even if it were there would be no eating facilities on board. Well used to the difficulties of getting from place to place in wartime, Maudie knew that it was wise to be prepared for anything.

★　★　★

'Oops! You've forgotten the kitchen sink!' Dick remarked, as he hefted Maudie's grip, pretending to stagger under the weight. 'Are you sure you wouldn't like to go back and fetch it?'

'Oh, you!' Maudie swung her handbag at him and missed. At that moment the taxi they had ordered drew up in front of her cottage and she climbed inside, with that feeling of anticipation that always accompanies setting off on holiday.

'Going on honeymoon, are we?' the driver asked.

'No,' said Maudie, and 'Yes,' said Dick, simultaneously.

This time her handbag found its mark and Dick rubbed his knee ruefully.

Through a friend of his in the police force, Dick had made a reservation for Maudie at a B & B in Liverpool. The landlady there had promised to find other accommodation for Dick somewhere in the neighbourhood. Having asked for directions at a newspaper kiosk on the station platform, they learned that they had a mile or two to walk, unless they caught a bus or hailed a taxi.

'It's hardly worth it,' Dick said. 'You can manage the walk, can't you, old girl?'

Maudie could. Years of cycling around the countryside in connection with her job had given her sturdy legs, and as long as Dick was there to carry her grip, she could manage very well. She was only thankful that her court shoes with their two-and-a-half-inch heels were stowed away in her grip. Her flat lace-ups might not be smart, but they were comfortable.

Although the war had been over for almost four years, the city still bore the scars of conflict. 'Poor old Liverpool,' Maudie mourned as they passed yet another bombsite. 'It's as bad as London. I really had no idea.'

'My chum told me it really took a pounding,' Dick agreed. 'It's because of the docks, you see. The Luftwaffe had a field day here. Oh, Green Street — this must be what we're looking for. Number 24, Nate said.'

A cheerful woman in a wraparound overall greeted them at the door. Pink curlers peeped from beneath her turban, showing strands of greying hair. 'Come inside. I expect you're ready for a cup of tea, aren't you, after coming all this way?

And you're going even further, aren't you, Constable? All the way to Canada! Fancy. A cousin of mine emigrated there last year. He's living in Vancouver now. Perhaps if I give you his address you can take him one of my fruitcakes? Always partial to a bit of my fruitcake was Albert, not that I could make one for him very often, what with rationing and all that.'

Dick told her tactfully that he was only going as far as Toronto and he doubted if he'd get the chance to visit Vancouver, which was almost three thousand miles away.

'I don't think she believed you,' Maudie whispered when they were sitting side by side on a horsehair sofa, waiting for the promised tea.

'People never do,' Dick said. 'It doesn't look so far on the map, you see.'

15

Mrs Marks explained that she didn't do suppers, which was what they had expected, so Maudie and Dick walked around the corner to a small restaurant the landlady had recommended. It just so happened that a cousin of hers ran it.

'You go to Vi and tell her I sent you. She'll do right by you,' she promised.

'More a café than a restaurant, I'd say,' Maudie grumbled, peering through the window at the small oilcloth-covered tables.

'As long as the food's edible I don't care,' Dick told her. 'I'm so hungry I could eat a horse. Just so long as they don't serve us watery boiled cabbage. I see enough of that in the police canteen.'

'It's all right for you, Dick Bryant! This time tomorrow you'll be eating off the fat of the land on that boat.'

'Don't you mean the fat of the sea?'

'Never you mind what I mean. I'm on

holiday. I was hoping for something special.'

'Come on; we'll have a look at the menu, and if we don't like the look of it we can go somewhere else.'

But they were reassured when they were given an effusive welcome by Cousin Vi, a cheerful woman who was as buxom as Mrs Marks was scrawny.

'I can do you some nice rissoles,' she told them. 'Homemade; none of them nasty shop-bought things. I ground up the rest of yesterday's roast beef to put in them. And how about runner beans and mashed potatoes? None of your tinned stuff! And what about some nice apple dumplings and custard to follow? I can see that you two don't worry about your waistlines!'

'What did she mean by that?' Dick hissed. 'Is she suggesting I'm fat?'

'Obviously she could see that the pair of us are in good condition,' Maudie told him and he relaxed, satisfied. Inwardly, however, she was fuming. She might be a little, well, *unsvelte,* if you wanted to put it that way, but she certainly hadn't let

129

herself go to seed, and if you were talking about an extra pound or two, well, Vi was a fine one to talk!

'What shall we do after we eat?' Dick asked. 'We could go to the pictures if there's anything interesting on. We could ask Vi. She might know.'

'It's a bit late for that,' Maudie told him. 'I always hate it when I get to the cinema halfway through the big picture, don't you? There doesn't seem much point if you miss the beginning. That sometimes happened when I was in training because of the unsociable hours we had to keep. There was only one thing worse, and that was missing the end because I didn't have a late pass. A waste of money, really, but I never could resist taking in a good film.'

'I understand from the brochure they gave us at the shipping office that we'll be treated to nightly film shows on board. All the latest releases, too. The ship has its own cinema, you know. None of those makeshift affairs like you get on film nights in church halls where the projector breaks down at the crucial moment!'

'And people start singing 'Why Are We Waiting',' Maudie agreed.

Long after they had finished their meal, which was excellent, Maudie and Dick sat at their table, discussing their future. No other customers came in, apart from a youth wanting change for half a crown so he could make a phone call from the kiosk up the road. Even when Vi dimmed the lights they failed to take the hint, and at last she had to come up to their table and request them to leave.

'Not that I want to interrupt love's young dream,' she told them, plonking their bill down in front of them, 'but I'm waiting to shut up shop. I don't live on the premises and I want to get on home.'

Dick brought out his wallet and extracted a pound note. 'That was an excellent meal, Mrs er . . . ' he told her. 'If you ever think of moving down to Midvale, we could get you a job in the police canteen. How about it?'

She laughed. 'My old man might have something to say about that! He works on the docks and I can't see him wanting to move down south.'

'Never mind him! Any woman who can cook like you can would soon catch herself another man in Midvale.'

'Get along with you!' she said, laughing as she picked up the money. 'Are you wanting change out of this, or do I get to scoop the lot as a token of your appreciation?'

'You were flirting, Dick Bryant!' Maudie said accusingly as they walked down the street, arm in arm.

'Was I? Never in this world. Just giving credit where credit is due. That's what makes the world go round.' Maudie kicked him lightly on the ankle.

★　★　★

The following morning saw them taking a taxi to the dock where Dick's ship was waiting. Maudie had left her luggage with Mrs Marks, for she had to spend a second night at the B & B before returning to Llandyfan.

She gasped when they arrived at the ship. Its sheer size was overwhelming. 'It's enormous, Dick! Why didn't you tell me?'

'I did!' he protested. '581.9 feet long; gross tonnage 20,488, with six steam turbines.'

'Which meant precisely nothing to me! The only part I remember is its speed. You said it could do 17.5 knots, whatever that means when it's at home.'

'You'll never make a sailor,' Dick told her. 'Nautical miles per hour, that's what.'

'That doesn't sound very fast to me.'

'Woman, I despair. Never mind the technical details. Let's go on board and have a look at my cabin.'

Dick showed his papers and his name was ticked off on a list. Maudie was welcomed as a visitor and was warned to leave as soon as the word was given, for fear of missing the chance to return safely to dry land. While they were standing in line she overheard a man reminiscing to his little boy.

'You won't remember this, Jimmy, because you were only a baby at the time, but you've actually sailed on this ship before.'

'Have I, Daddy?'

'She was called the *Duchess of Bedford*

133

then. It was just before the fall of Singapore and the ship had just arrived there with hundreds of troops and a group of nurses. Then you and Mummy and hundreds of other refugees boarded this very ship and were taken away to safety.'

'Were you on it too, Daddy?'

'I'm afraid not. I was taken prisoner by the Japanese and I didn't come back to Britain until you were quite a big boy. Don't you remember?'

The queue moved forward then and Maudie heard no more, but she was impressed. She had come through a war herself and knew about many of the deeds of heroism performed by servicemen and woman as well as members of the public. But this was the first time she'd thought of ships as having played a vital role, as of course they had.

She followed Dick as he made his way to the cabin where he was to spend the next six days. She found it rather delightful, with its two bunks and everything else that fitted neatly into its compact space. Wardrobe, chest of drawers and dressing table were all there, as well as an armchair and a matching padded stool. She was amused by the porthole, which was supplied with curtains made of the same fabric as the bedspreads.

'Who on earth could peer in, a mermaid?' she said, giggling, feeling silly when Dick pointed out that many of the portholes overlooked a passageway on the deck, if that was the right term for a sort of hallway from which passengers could reach their cabins or walk to other parts of the ship.

She was impressed by the dining room, with its tables for six or eight people. The snowy white tablecloths and gleaming silverware and vases of flowers would not have disgraced the Ritz Hotel; not that she had ever set foot inside the Ritz! The lounge, card room and bar were equally magnificent. If all this was for tourist-class passengers, what could first-class accommodations be like? The *Empress of France* was like a magnificent floating hotel.

A siren blew. A disembodied voice boomed over a speaker: 'All ashore that's going ashore!'

'I thought it only happened like that in films,' she said.

'This is it, then,' Dick said, turning to sweep her into his arms. Maudie clung to him as if they were about to bid each other goodbye forever. Their kiss seemed to last for a very long time, and then she broke away and headed blindly towards the way out, unaware that Dick was close behind her, anxious for her safety.

She soon found herself at the dockside, jockeying for position so she could see what was happening on board. People of all shapes and sizes crowded the ship's rail, waving and calling to those who had come to see them off. Dick might have been among them, but Maudie's vision was blurred by tears. What sounded like a foghorn assailed her ears, and the giant vessel was ready to set sail.

16

Mrs Marks was inclined to be chatty. Maudie was the only guest there for breakfast, and the landlady's husband had already left for work. Accepting scrambled eggs on toast and declining sausage, bacon and black pudding, Maudie let the chit-chat flow over her head.

'Are you sure you won't have a nice fry-up, love? You want to keep your strength up with all those trains you've got to catch today. Fancy, two changes, and then another taxi ride. Worn out you'll be before you get to bed tonight. No? You better have another cuppa then, good and strong with plenty of sugar to keep you going.'

'I'd like the tea, please, but only one sugar. I don't want to put on any weight before my wedding of I'll have to go to the altar dressed in a sack!'

Mrs Marks's ears pricked up. 'A wedding! You're getting married! Oh, that's grand, that is. Is it your first time, love?'

'Yes, that's right.'

'I must say, your chap seems a good sort. But he's gone to Canada without you. Will he be coming back?'

'Oh, I do hope so. He hasn't emigrated, you see; he's just gone over there to do with his job.'

'He's a bobby, isn't he? Oh, he will look fine in those red coats they wear, and the big cowboy hat. Will he wear the uniform to get married in? You'll have to find something really fancy to wear or he'll leave you in the shade!'

'No, no. You're thinking of the Mounties, the Royal Canadian Mounted Police. Ordinary policemen in Canada usually wear navy blue uniforms, or so I've been told. They probably look a lot like our men, except they don't wear the same helmets.'

'It's such a shame you couldn't have got married before he left, or you could have gone with him.'

'Actually that's what Dick wanted me to do, but I decided to wait. There's my job, you see. I couldn't leave people in the lurch.'

'A secretary, are you?'

'No, I'm a midwife.'

Mrs Marks stared at Maudie, wrinkling her nose. 'Oh, I don't think I'd fancy that myself. I come over all queer at the sight of blood. I just know I'd faint when I saw the baby arriving. Still, it's useful work, and I suppose somebody has to do it.'

'It suits me,' Maudie said. 'I can't say I'd fancy running a B & B myself.'

'Whyever not? It's money for jam, really. As long as you put a good breakfast on the table and put fresh linen on the beds, that's it for the day. Your time is your own until they come back at bedtime. That's if people are staying more than one night, like yourself.'

'Oh, surely there's more to it than that. Don't you have to clean the house, do laundry, scrub the doorstep, go out shopping for food supplies and all that?'

The woman looked at Maudie as if she was mad. 'Well, of course, but that's just regular housework, isn't it? You'd do that even if you weren't running a business, so it doesn't count.'

'Yes, I suppose you would,' Maudie said. 'It's different in my line of work, you see. Aside from making my rounds in the district, and seeing people in the office, I'm liable to be called out at any time of day or night. I'm afraid I have to fit my chores around all that. I do try to keep my cottage clean, of course, but it's difficult to stick to a regular routine, such as you must do.'

'You'll feel the draught when you get married, then,' Mrs. Marks told her sternly. 'Your hubby will expect to come home to a clean and tidy house, with a good meal waiting to go on the table. How are you going to manage then?'

'That's why nurses have to give up work when they marry, Mrs Marks, and I expect that will apply to me, too, although to be honest I'm not sure where I stand in that regard. That will have to be looked into. Hospital nurses aren't allowed to work after they marry because the hours are just too long to accommodate married life. Night shifts are usually twelve hours long, and the day shifts run for thirteen hours with a three-hour break somewhere in the middle.'

'Slavery, that's what is,' the landlady observed.

When she was probationer in the big hospital where she had gone to train, Maudie had thought so too. After a long day on the wards she could barely find the energy to soak her tired feet in a mustard bath before she fell into bed. Yet she would not have changed her lot for all the world. When you found something you loved doing you were prepared to work all hours at it. She knew now that this applied to everything in life, whether it was paid work or some entrancing hobby.

★ ★ ★

Without Dick to talk to, the return journey to Llandyfan seemed to last forever. Standing on the platform at Lime Street station, Maudie had become thoroughly chilled in the damp morning air, and by the time she had manhandled her suitcase onto the train she felt quite dispirited. She was beginning to learn that a middle-aged woman is practically invisible when it comes to finding waiters, taxis or other so-called helpful personnel, and the railway porters bore out her findings. Or was it because she looked shabby in her gabardine raincoat, and thus unlikely to come up with a substantial tip for services rendered?

The women's magazine she had purchased from the kiosk on the platform failed to interest her. The knitting pattern depicted the sort of garment she would never wear, and the cookery recipes called for ingredients she would never use. As for the fashions, dear me! Did dress designers ever keep real women in mind when they thought up such outlandish wear?

When at long last she transferred to the small cross-country train, things began to look up. She found herself in a compartment with a mother and a very young baby, and when the child began to wail, refusing to be comforted, Maudie was in her element.

'May I try?' she asked. 'I'm a midwife,

so I do know something about babies.'

The grateful young woman handed her little boy into Maudie's expert hands with a sigh of relief. Moments later he gave a resounding burp, which made them laugh. Then he fell asleep. The rest of the journey seemed to pass in a flash, as Maudie willingly answered the girl's questions about childcare.

The final stage of her journey was on a small local train, which seemed to stop at every halt and junction. At long last she sank into the taxi she'd pre-ordered, and was whisked to Llandyfan.

When she was deposited at her cottage gate she was beyond tiredness. It was as if she had returned from a trip to the moon, so distant did Liverpool seem to her now. And what, she wondered, was Dick up to? Was he having a fine time sitting in the bar, talking to his colleagues, or playing cards in that ornate saloon set aside for the purpose? Or was he perhaps missing her as much as she yearned for him and was already beginning the letter he had promised her?

The house felt strangely empty when

she deposited her suitcase inside the front door. She'd been looking forward to a hot bath, some tea and toast, and then collapsing into her very own bed, but now she seemed to have got her second wind. Perhaps it would be a good idea to pop over to the vicarage to let Mrs Blunt know she was back, although she must stress that she was still off duty. She didn't want to be called out to some emergency during the small hours.

''Oh, Nurse, you're back!' Mrs Blunt cried, greeting Maudie with what, for her, was a very glum expression on her face. 'Such terrible news, isn't it?'

Maudie's heart gave a lurch. Had something happened to the *Empress of France* that she was unaware of? But they had been at sea for less than two days. Surely they could not have met an iceberg yet! 'It's not Dick, is it?' she quavered. 'Has something gone wrong with the ship? Has there been something on the wireless? Please, please don't keep me in suspense, Mrs Blunt. I must know the worst!'

Mrs Blunt looked contrite. 'No, no, Nurse. I didn't mean to alarm you. I'm sure all is well with the ship, and with Constable Bryant, too. If you've only just arrived home, then I suppose you won't have heard.'

'Heard what? Is it one of my patients? Has someone miscarried?'

'About the murder, Nurse. There's been another murder, right here in Llandyfan.'

17

'Oh, not again!' Maudie wailed. 'Who has been killed? Anybody we know?'

'I'm afraid it's Miss Mason,' Mrs Blunt told her. 'Dr Lennox's fiancée.'

'She wasn't his fiancée,' Maudie said automatically. 'But what happened to her? Where was she found?'

'It seems she was killed on Mrs Beasley's estate. There's a tumbledown hut on the other side of the copse and that's where it happened, apparently. She seems to have been given a heavy blow to the back of the head, although I don't think they've found the murder weapon yet.'

'If she was killed in such a remote place I'm surprised the poor woman was found so soon,' Maudie mused. 'It's not as though the place is overrun with game-keepers, like the old days. And what was she doing there in the first place, so far off the beaten track?'

'Nobody seems to know,' Mrs Blunt said, shaking her head. 'Possibly she was lured there by the murderer. And it was the Scouts who found her. Mrs Beasley had given the troop permission to use that part of the property for what they call a wide game. Something to do with maps and compasses, I gather. When they came upon the hut, two of the boys decided to hide from the rest so they went inside. And that's when they found the body. I was talking to the mother of one of the lads and she told me that they thought at first it was all part of the exercise they were on and they were meant to administer first aid to a pretend victim. Then one of the boys touched the back of Miss Mason's head and realised he had real blood on his fingers.'

'Poor kid.'

'And of course the police have been crawling all over the place ever since; looking for clues, I suppose, or whatever it is they have to do.'

'And are there any suspects?'

Mrs Blunt bit her lip. 'Well, that's the awful thing, Nurse! Dr Lennox has been accused. They've taken him away for questioning. 'Helping the police with their enquiries.' That's how the newspapers love to describe it, isn't it?'

Maudie's jaw dropped. She listened in a daze as her friend continued with her story. 'There has to be some dreadful mistake, Nurse. He seems to be such a lovely young man, devoting all his time to his patients, and treating everyone in such a kindly manner. Now he's not only lost his fiancée, but he's been accused of killing her as well. I feel so sorry for him.'

'Yes,' Maudie murmured, but her thoughts whirled in her tired brain. Was she the only one who knew that Paula had been threatening to take him to court, to sue him over what — according to him, at least — was the breaking of a non-existent engagement?

A theory began to build in her mind. Dr Lennox had agreed to meet Paula. He had chosen a remote spot so that curious passers-by could not overhear them. He had stood up to her, but she would not be reasoned with, and had persisted in her demands. She had turned to leave, saying that she was more than ever determined to carry on with her plan. In a moment of fury he had picked up the — what? — and hit her over the head. Then, aghast at what he had done, he hurried away, leaving her lying on the ground.

And this, Maudie realised, was partly her fault, because hadn't she advised the doctor to have it out with the girl? She began to shake, only partly from the fatigue and cold that were catching up with her.

'Nurse! Are you all right?'

Maudie came out of her daydream to find Mrs Blunt looking at her with concern. 'Oh, sorry! I was miles away. Look, I'd better go home. We can talk about it tomorrow.'

'Of course. You must be exhausted after travelling all day. Why not pop in for morning coffee? I'm dying to hear all about Dick's ship.'

* * *

Maudie went about her preparations for bed in a robot-like fashion. Murder

149

seemed to follow her around. Two years ago she had actually discovered the body when a man had been throttled, up on the hillside above the Bassett farm. The poor chap had come to Llandyfan in search of the granddaughter he had never known, the child of his only son who had been killed on active service during the war.

Then, only last year, Maudie had been instrumental in finding the killer of Madam Zora, the fortuneteller who had been strangled in her tent at the church fête. On that occasion Maudie had almost become a victim herself when the man had followed her into the churchyard at night. Only the presence of a pair of young lovers had saved her then.

Now it seemed that she was about to be involved again. Was it her duty to go to the police with what Dr Lennox had told her? But that would only drop him in it? Because it did seem like an obvious motive for getting rid of Paula. She wished that Dick were here to advise her.

She tossed and turned all night, eventually dropping off to sleep when the first signs of a rosy dawn appeared in the sky. It seemed like only moments later that she was jerked out of sleep by the insistent ringing of the telephone at her bedside.

'Go away!' she muttered, pulling the pillow over her head. But the jangling tones continued, and at last she snatched up the receiver, knocking over her water glass in the process.

'Who is it?' she barked. 'What time is it?'

'There is no need to take that tone with me, Nurse. And as for the time, it's gone seven. Time you were up and about and preparing for the day's work.'

Dr Dean, her nemesis! Maudie took a deep breath. 'You'll have to excuse me, Doctor. I've just returned from Liverpool and I was travelling all day yesterday. And I'm not back on duty until tomorrow.'

'That can't be helped. You'll have to pull yourself together and get up to Dr Lennox's surgery. I don't know if you've heard, but he's been arrested. Someone will have to deal with the patients, who I'm sure will be turning up in droves.'

'But can't you . . . '

'No, I certainly cannot. I have my own surgery to see to, here in Midvale.'

'But the doctor's cousin, Mr Munroe, will be there. Surely he can deal with people.'

'He's only a glorified receptionist. You'll have to handle this situation, Nurse Rouse. Sort out the sheep from the goats. Yes, I'm aware that you're only a midwife, but surely even you can manage to advise those with the odd cough or sniffle or a minor rash. Keep a list of anything urgent and report back to me after lunch. Now, have I made myself clear?'

'Quite clear, Doctor,' Maudie snapped, but he had gone and she found herself speaking to dead air. Bristling with indignation, she replaced the earpiece on its hook and swung her feet over the side of the bed. Only a midwife indeed!

'Bang goes my day off!' she muttered. She had so looked forward to a pleasant day of doing nothing much: visiting Mrs Blunt for coffee and perhaps having a nice walk in the fresh air. Now she had to struggle into her uniform and cycle the two miles over to Dr Lennox's surgery.

On the other hand, she thought, brightening, this gave her the perfect excuse to find out what was going on with the police investigation. It might be worth giving up her day off after all.

★ ★ ★

'What are you doing here?' Bingo Munroe demanded, in charming greeting.

'I've come to take the surgery while Dr Lennox is away,' she informed him.

'Have you, indeed! We'll see what Dr Dean has to say about that.'

'It was Dr Dean who sent me here. He has his own surgery to take care of. Now then, I don't think it will be necessary for you to stay, Mr Munroe, so perhaps you'd like to take the day off?'

'I must be here to announce the patients as they come in, Nurse.'

'That won't be necessary, Mr Munroe. I believe I know everyone who is likely to come. I've brought most of their children into the world, you see. Besides, won't your aunt need you up at the house? She must be in great distress after what has happened.'

'Oh, yes,' he said, half-closing his eyes as if in deep thought. 'It's quite a shock for dear Auntie, finding out that her blue-eyed boy isn't all he's made himself out to be!'

Maudie stared at him, dumbfounded. She had already gathered that there wasn't much love lost between the cousins, but this was going too far. Bingo was living under his aunt's roof and had been given a job by her, such as it was. She assumed that he was being paid for his work, but even if he wasn't he was getting board and lodging which, presumably, he didn't have to pay for. As far as Maudie knew he had come for Christmas and stayed on. Now it was the middle of April and he was still here. Didn't the man know the meaning of gratitude?

'I'm off, then,' he announced, his harsh voice breaking in on her thoughts. 'If anyone wants me I'll be in the Royal Oak.'

'They won't be serving yet,' Maudie reminded him.

'Some of the locals get together in the morning for a game of dominoes,' Bingo informed her. 'Not that it's any of your business, Nurse.' He walked away, letting the door swing shut behind him.

18

Maudie went into the little consulting room and looked about her. She noticed a small blackboard fixed to the wall beside Dr Lennox's chair, with something written on it in spidery handwriting. A closer inspection proved that it had to do with requests for home visits; apparently Bingo had made a note of requests that had come in for the doctor.

There was only one. 'Mrs Harry Dempster', it said. 'Baby with wracking cough'. That would be little Grace, Maudie realised. She had delivered the child herself some months previously, and in fact the baby was named after her, Grace being her middle name. Well, no problem there. She would call in on her way home and see what was to be done.

Meanwhile, there were the walking wounded to be dealt with. When the clock chimed the hour she entered the waiting room, which was full to overflowing.

'Good morning, all!'

A chorus of 'morning, Nurse' came in response, accompanied by a few coughs and groans.

'I'm afraid the doctor can't see you today,' she began. 'He's been called away.'

'Aye, and we all know why!'

She ignored the burly man in the front row and carried on. 'Now then, if any of you have complaints that can possibly wait, I'll ask you to come back another time, please.'

'When's he coming back, then?'

'I'm afraid I don't know. Meanwhile, I'm filling in for him, so as I said, I'd like those of you with nothing pressing to leave, please. I'll see everyone else and decide what's best to be done. All right?'

There were dissatisfied mumbles, but to her relief several people got up and left, including the belligerent man. She prayed that she hadn't done the wrong thing, but she couldn't possibly have dealt with these numbers unaided, and in any case she suspected that some people had only come out of curiosity, citing vague aches and pains as an excuse.

Maudie dealt with the remaining patients in short order. There was one man who was convinced he was about to be floored by a heart attack, but she put his discomfort down to acute indigestion after asking a few pertinent questions. He admitted to eating a mound of fried onions after downing one two many tankards of ale in the Royal Oak, and after giving a resounding burp that nearly blew Maudie off her chair, he agreed that she must be right. 'Bicarb,' she told him. 'That's the answer.'

'Yes, Nurse, I expect you're right.'

'Mind you,' she warned him, well aware that she was not a doctor and so not qualified to make a diagnosis, 'you must come and consult Dr Lennox very soon, just to make sure. Will you do that, Mr Soper?'

'If you think it's necessary, Nurse. But do you think he will be coming back? To listen to the talk that's doing the rounds it sounds like he's accused of bumping off that young woman.'

'Oh, no, he's just been called in to help the police because he's known her for years,' Maudie replied, for the umpteenth time. 'They have to know about her next of kin and all that, and he's the one to fill them in. They can save themselves a lot of time by picking his brains.'

'Is that so?'

'Absolutely. Now, if the bicarb doesn't work, you can always go to see Dr Dean, and of course you can request a house call if you really feel unwell.'

'Right-ho, Nurse. Thanks.'

Maudie inspected a nasty case of contact dermatitis, bound up a sprained ankle accompanied by words of wisdom about how to treat it at home, and discussed the treatment of nappy rash. The only patient with a potentially serious condition was a woman complaining of pains in her right side. It was plain to see that she fell in the category of 'fair, fat and forty', which pointed to gall bladder trouble or gallstones. While reassuring the patient that she wasn't in imminent danger, Maudie stressed that a doctor must evaluate the condition. Should she call an ambulance and ship the patient to the cottage hospital? No, that hardly seemed necessary.

'I feel that you ought to pop over to Midvale and have a word with Dr Dean,' she said. 'There's a bus in half an hour so why not go this morning? There's no point in putting it off.'

'Oh, him! Do I really have to?'

'Yes, you do,' Maudie said firmly. She would look silly if Dr Lennox returned soon, yet she didn't want to find herself in trouble if the woman's condition worsened. Nor, of course, did she want the patient to suffer unnecessarily. She would phone Dr Dean later to make sure that the woman had indeed consulted him, and if she had not, she would ask him to make a house call. She wouldn't be popular, but that was what he was paid for!

At last the rush was over. Maudie sat at Dr Lennox's desk, making a neat copy of her own scrawled notes to leave for him. She would take her own notes away with her, just in case there were any questions later.

The outer door creaked. She got her from her chair, filled with relief. 'Is that you, Dr Lennox?'

'No, Nurse, it's only me.'

The imposing figure of Cora Beasley filled the doorway. Maudie had met her at church events but had never come to know her socially.

'Oh, Mrs Beasley! Do come in and sit down.' Maudie realised, too late, that she had probably said the wrong thing. The former gatehouse and everything else on the estate belonged to this woman. It was hardly the done thing to invite her to sit down in her own place!

Fortunately the lady didn't seem to notice anything amiss. Sinking down in the patients' chair, she regarded Maudie with a woeful expression on her chubby face. 'I suppose you've heard what's going on with my nephew, Nurse Rouse?'

'Well, I . . . '

'There's no need to pussyfoot around, Nurse. I know what's being said in the village, and it's only going to get worse. I thought I'd better pop down to see how you're managing. I can't get any sense out of Brian. He muttered something about a nurse being here, and now he's sulking in his bedroom.'

'Brian?' Oh, of course! That was Bingo's rightful name.

'Brian Munroe, my useless nephew! Oh, don't listen to me, Nurse. I know it's not the done thing to wash one's dirty linen in public, but just between us he's always been a waste of space, and now he's become a thorn in my side!'

Fighting words indeed, Maudie thought. She tried to come up with words of consolation, and failed. 'If there's anything I can do . . . '

Mrs Beasley sighed. 'As long as you can hold the fort, Nurse, that's all anyone can ask.'

'Can't Bingo — er — Mr Munroe answer the telephone at least, Mrs Beasley? I really must get over to the Dempsters' house. They asked for Dr Lennox to make a house call to see little Grace.'

'Not while he's in this mood. Perhaps if you speak to Miss Gunn at the Exchange, she'll reroute Leonard's calls to your home or office. How will that do?'

Maudie hesitated. 'Certainly, Mrs Beasley, but does this mean you're not expecting Dr Lennox back any time soon?'

The older woman leaned over, resting her chin on one fist before replying. Then she straightened, looking defiantly at Maudie. 'They've arrested him, Nurse! They've charged my nephew with the murder of that unfortunate young woman. It's utterly ridiculous, of course, as they're bound to find out in the end; but meanwhile we must try to keep the ship afloat, wouldn't you agree?'

'Of course. I'll do everything I can to help.'

It occurred to Maudie that it might be best to have all the calls put through to Dr Dean, but that would be hard on any of the patients who had minor complaints which could easily be dealt with by a nurse. And, much as she disliked Dr Dean, it would be unprofessional of her to add to his workload unnecessarily. Besides, if all calls were routed through her, that was one way of keeping her finger on the pulse of what was bring said and done in Llandyfan.

She was uncomfortably aware that even if Dr Lennox were exonerated, this nasty business would do him no good at all professionally. No smoke without fire, that was what the locals would say, and who could blame them? Until the killer was found and taken into custody, Dr Lennox's good name would be tarnished.

Maddy Gunn, of course, would be only too pleased to listen in to everything that was said, but that was nothing new. It was common knowledge that the girls on the switchboard listened in avidly, even going so far as to alert their colleagues if something interesting cropped up. As a result, people were used to speaking in a sort of code.

One good thing about the medical profession was the jargon used by doctors and nurses. Maudie could speak to Dr Dean in words that the listeners could not readily understand, and thus preserve some semblance of patient confidentiality.

19

Maudie could hear baby Grace's harsh cough even before she rapped lightly on the kitchen door of Phyllis Dempster's house. Phyllis herself answered the door, holding the baby on her hip. It was obvious that the child was struggling for breath. Peering out from behind their mother's skirts were two older children, both of primary school age.

'Oh, Nurse, thank goodness! Is Dr Lennox on his way? Harry was supposed to take a message on his way to work this morning, but the doctor never came.'

'I'm here now, Phyllis. Shall I come in?' Maudie pushed past the anxious mother who was dithering in the doorway.

'Just listen to her, Nurse! I've been so worried! Is it whooping cough? Is it diphtheria? Will she have to go into hospital?'

'It's croup,' Maudie announced, taking the child into her own arms. 'And by the look of it these other two are home with colds. Am I right?' The little girl nodded. Her brother wiped his nose on his sleeve, leaving a silvery trail on the wool.

'How many times have I told you to use your hankie, Bobby Dempster?' his mother cried. 'Why do you think you've got that thing pinned to your front, eh?' The teachers at the local school insisted that all the youngsters kept a hankie pinned to their persons, even if it was nothing but a piece of old rag. The trick lay in persuading the newest pupils to use them.

Maudie smiled at the children. 'Now then, Phyllis. Bring out the biggest pots you can find, fill them with water and put them on the cooker to boil. We want to get up a good head of steam in the room. You'll need to keep that going night and day for a while. Not at full blast, of course; you can let it simmer as long as the steam keeps coming. When that's done I want you to bring the baby's cot downstairs. You'll have to keep it here in the kitchen until she's over this bout.'

Half an hour later, with all these refinements in place, Maudie sat down at the kitchen table with Grace on her lap. The baby was already beginning to breathe more easily and her mother was visibly relaxed.

'How do you like school, Bobby?' Maudie knew that the little lad was in his first year there.

'I like the plasticine,' he said shyly.

'He doesn't like the two times tables,' his sister chipped in.

'And Mummy doesn't like these colds you bring home,' Maudie said. 'It's always the way when the kiddies first start at school, Phyllis. Colds and things go all round the class like lightning.'

'Just as long as it's not chicken pox or that,' Phyllis said. 'Do you reckon our Grace will be okay now? I'll keep the steam coming like you said.' She brushed a film of moisture off her forehead and Maudie's own face felt damp.

'I'd best be going, Phyllis, but I'll be talking to Dr Dean on the telephone later this afternoon and I'll find out if he wants to prescribe something for Grace. All right?'

'Thanks, Nurse.'

'And why waste all that lovely steam? Perhaps you could make a jam roly-poly while you're at it.' She grinned and went on her way.

★ ★ ★

Maudie looked in at the rectory to see Mrs Blunt. 'I'm on my way home; I haven't come to stop. I just wanted to let you know that Dr Lennox is still not back, so anyone in trouble should contact me directly, and I'll take it from there.'

'I see. And when will the doctor be returning? Has anyone told you?'

Maudie leaned closer to her friend. 'I don't suppose this will remain a secret for very long, but in the meantime we'd better keep this between ourselves. According to his aunt, the doctor has been arrested and charged with the murder of Paula Mason.'

'No!'

'I'm afraid so, Mrs Blunt.'

'But do you think it's true? Oh, I don't mean what she told you; Cora Beasley wouldn't lie. But what motive would the man have for killing that girl? They were

168

supposed to be engaged, weren't they?'

'That was all in her mind, apparently. They've known each other for years and he did take the girl out once or twice, but there was never any more to it than that.'

'How do you know all this, Nurse?' Mrs Blunt said, her eyes wide.

'Because Dr Lennox told me so himself. What it amounts to is the girl had been stalking him, threatening to sue him for breach of promise. He came to ask my advice about it some days ago, and I told him to seek the advice of a solicitor.'

'You didn't tell me this before.'

'I couldn't. It was said to me in confidence. Now, though, I suppose it all has to come out, and one way or the other it means the poor man is finished in the medical profession, which of course is what she wanted.'

Mrs Blunt sighed. 'The barristers will have a field day with this when it comes to trial. And as you say, even if he gets off, what patient will ever trust him again?'

They heard a door open and close. The Reverend Harold Blunt entered the room, looking sad.

'How did you find Mrs Lester, dear?' his wife murmured.

'She's gone, Joan. I'm so thankful I was there with her at the end, to provide her with the consolation of her faith. To think I almost didn't go when the summons came. I'm ashamed to say I felt quite annoyed at the thought of being dragged away from my crossword puzzle, when this time she really was dying.'

'Poor old soul. Well, at ninety-seven it was only to be expected, and you've been very faithful in attendance, dear, even when you've been sent for at two o'clock in the morning.'

'Of course that son of hers was there. Not that he shouldn't have been, when his mother was dying. It's just that he's such a bully, talking to me as if I were a naughty schoolboy, up on the carpet in front of the headmaster. He says he sent for her doctor but the doctor didn't bother to come. Not the sort of behaviour he's been used to, apparently.'

'I dread to think what he'll say when he finds out why,' Mrs Blunt said. 'Nurse has just been telling me, Harold. Dr Lennox has been arrested for the murder of poor Miss Mason.'

'Oh, dear! Then I suppose I must pop over to see Cora Beasley. This will hit her hard, I know. By the way, Nurse, before I forget: Lester would like you to go the house and lay his mother out. Can you manage that?'

'I'll go over now, then. No point in putting it off.'

*   *   *

'And I might as well go over to the big house before I put the car away,' the vicar said. 'I wonder if I should telephone first, to let Mrs Beasley know I'm on my way?'

'I don't believe that would be necessary, dear,' his wife told him. 'Would you like me to come with you?'

'It might be a good idea for us to present a united front. After all, she is the president of the Mothers' Union.'

'And I'm the vicar's wife,' Joan, said, smiling. 'Can you wait five minutes? I must just run upstairs and change my frock. I've been cleaning out the bedroom cupboards in this one, and it looks it.'

'You look very nice, dear,' her husband told her. 'But then you always look nice to me.'

'Thank you for the compliment, Harold, but I still think I'd better tidy myself up a bit.' She pulled a face at Maudie, who raised her eyebrows in return. Men!

Wearily Maudie went out and retrieved her bicycle, casting a longing glance at her cottage as she passed by. Thoughts of hot scented bath water, hot sweet tea and a perusal of her weekly magazine went through her mind and faded away again. Duty called.

★ ★ ★

The old lady lay on her bed, arms folded across the snowy white bedspread covering her chest. Maudie paused for a moment before beginning her task. Even in death Mrs Lester deserved the same consideration that she would have received in life. There would be no rush, no lack of dignity while these last offices were performed. She would be treated with as much respect as if she were still alive and able to protest at what was being done to her. Maudie fetched a basin of warm water from the bathroom and opened the pack she had brought with her from her office in the parish hall. Gently and reverently she bent to her task.

20

'You've got a postcard, Nurse.' Maudie could see that the postmistress was holding up a card that bore a coloured picture of the *Empress of France*. 'It's from your hubby-to-be,' Mrs Hatch went on. 'He says, 'Having a wonderful time. Wish you were here. Love, Dick.' Isn't that sweet!'

Annoyed, Maudie said, 'Why wasn't that delivered to me instead of left sitting here for just anyone to read?'

She was rewarded with a bland stare. 'Because it just arrived, that's why. I'm sorting the post now, aren't I? Of course, if you'd rather wait and have it delivered tomorrow morning it makes no odds to me.'

'Oh, give it here!' Maudie reached out and snatched it, none too gently. She'd been hoping to hear from Dick for days now. Where was the newsy letter she'd been promised?

Mrs Hatch nodded. 'Have you heard the latest? Old Mrs Lester died.'

'I know, thank you very much. I've just finished laying her out, and now I've come for a tin of soup because I don't feel like cooking after the day I've had.'

'Ah! I heard you had to take Dr Lennox's surgery for him. Martha Brown was in here, saying she went all the way up there and then she had to come away because she reckoned there was nothing you could do for her bunions. And as for Gladys Rees, well! Proper cross she was, on account of you told her she shouldn't have plastered butter on that burnt hand of hers, where she caught it on the iron. She'll go to Dr Dean the next time, she says.'

'Good luck to her then!' Maudie snapped. 'And I'd like to be a fly on the wall when Dr Dean tells her what he thinks of her burn ointment. She'll get her come-uppance then.'

'No need to be like that, Nurse. Everyone knows it's butter you use for burns, and goose grease for bad chests.'

'I approve of goose grease and a good

layer of brown paper for a winter chest,' Maudie said, 'but butter for a burn is completely wrong, and you can tell them all I said so!' She marched out of the shop, completely forgetting the tin of mulligatawny she'd hoped to find.

'Well! Whatever has got into her?' Mrs Hatch asked, to nobody in particular.

Truth to tell, Maudie was thoroughly fed up. She had done her best to accommodate the doctor's patients and she thought she'd done rather well, even if she was 'only a nurse' as one man had informed her, under the impression that he was paying her a compliment.

She could have done without having to prepare old Mrs Lester for burial, because she had given her back a painful wrench while attempting to turn the deceased lady on her side. Had she been in a hospital setting she would have had another nurse to assist her, but in Llandyfan there was nobody available. She could hardly ask the bereaved son to play a part in the proceedings, even though a female relative might have been expected to help.

Then she couldn't get Dr Lennox out of her mind. Had he killed Paula Mason? If a jury found him guilty, he would hang. In England jurors had only two choices: to find an accused person guilty or not guilty. Maudie wished that the trial could take place in Scotland, for they had a third option there; a verdict of not proven was possible.

It was terrible to think that in just a few weeks young Dr Lennox might be dead, and what a waste that would be, and what a loss to the medical community. Imagine spending all those years studying and slaving away in hospitals, only to be cut off in one's prime.

But of course if he really had committed murder, then he must pay the price. But how hard it would be for his family, who would forever bear the terrible grief and shame of the crime he had committed. And what about the grief of Paula Mason's people, whoever they might be, a little voice reminded Maudie.

★ ★ ★

177

That evening she went for a walk to clear her head. Everywhere she went, birds were chirping and singing; and as she walked down a country lane she was charmed to see a pair of rabbits chasing each other. All the world seemed to be pairing off, and she was reminded that she was now part of a couple herself. That certainly gave her spirits a lift.

Strolling towards her favourite spot on the river, she was rather annoyed to find a man standing on the bank in the very place where she had meant to sit down. In past years she had observed kingfishers there and she hoped to see them again. She doubted if they would show themselves if there were people about.

Coming closer, she recognised the man as Bingo Munroe. He seemed to be staring into space and he gave no sign that he knew he wasn't alone. She hoped he wasn't thinking of doing away with himself, for he didn't seemed to be bird-watching. But if he just wanted an evening stroll in the country, why come all the way out here? His aunt had an extensive estate that was full of meadows and woods where he might wander at will. She felt instinctively that something was wrong here. She quickened her pace and joined him.

'Mr Munroe! It's me, Nurse Rouse. Are you all right?'

He twisted around to face her so quickly that she took a step backwards in alarm.

'No, of course I'm not all right!' he snapped. 'And I'll thank you to leave me alone! It's coming to something if a man can't come out for a bit of peace and quiet without being accosted by all and sundry, wanting to know if I'm all right!'

'I know you must be worried about your cousin,' Maudie said softly. 'We must just hope that everything turns out for the best.'

'Oh, Leo Lennox deserves all that's coming to him!' Bingo said, his tone full of bitterness. 'Everything has always been handed to him on a plate, not like some! Born into a family where he was given everything he ever wanted; all the latest toys, new shoes every year, no hand-me-downs for him! Then off to the best schools, followed by university and medical school! Some people have all the luck, living off the fat of the land while the rest of us are left to struggle on.'

'Life does seem unfair at times,' Maudie murmured.

'Unfair! Let me tell you what's unfair, Nurse! Not only does my cousin have all that, but then good old Auntie shells out even more! She's had that gatehouse done up for him at great expense and she's helped to fund his buying into a medical practice. When is it going to be my turn, eh?'

'I'm sure your turn will come, Mr Munroe.'

'Are you! Well, perhaps you're right. With the blue-eyed boy out of the way perhaps I'll get a look-in.'

Despite the warmth of the evening, Maudie felt a chill go through her. She could understand his envy of his more fortunate cousin, but this was downright jealousy. The man could not be in his right mind if he could view the probable execution of Dr Lennox, his own flesh and blood, with such glee.

As if reading her thoughts, Bingo regarded her with narrowed eyes. 'I suppose you think he should get off! You women are all the same. You can't see past his film-star good looks to the evil underneath. He's a cold-blooded killer who did away with Paula Mason. Somebody has to pay for that, don't you think?'

'Well, the poor girl certainly didn't deserve to die,' Maudie murmured, wondering how she could extricate herself from this unpleasant conversation.

'You don't know what you're talking about, Nurse Rouse! That girl was rotten to the core, like all women! If Leo hadn't got rid of her, someone else would have done away with her eventually. That's how it works, you see.'

He stepped away from Maudie then and, open-mouthed, she watched him stride away in the direction of the village. All her pleasure in the delights of the spring evening evaporated as she considered what she had just heard. She wished fervently that Dick were here to discuss this with her, but he was far away, not even reachable by telephone. She needed to talk to someone about this strange encounter, however, so, her mind made up, she made her way to the rectory.

The vicar and his wife listened quietly while Maudie told her story.

'How unpleasant for you, Nurse,' Mrs Blunt murmured.

'I suppose I shouldn't have interfered,' Maudie admitted, 'but him standing there like a beanpole gave me the creeps. I was afraid he might do away with himself, you see.'

'I don't think we should read too much into this,' the vicar said. 'This is for your ears only, Nurse, and I shouldn't really be sharing this information, but under the circumstances, well . . . I called on Mrs Beasley today and she tells me she's thinking of selling up and moving to a retirement home. She feels she cannot face staying on here with all that has happened.'

'That's quite understandable.'

'Yes indeed. And I don't think she's thought very far beyond that at present, but no doubt Mr Munroe is wondering where this leaves him.'

'I should think it leaves him where the rest of us are,' Maudie said sternly. She had no time for malingerers. 'He'll have to look for a job like everyone else, and just get on with it.'

'Ah, if only life were so simple, Nurse,' the vicar said sadly. 'But human nature being what it is, we cannot expect everyone to feel as you do. And I'm afraid that life has not treated Mr Munroe with the same kindness that has been Dr Lennox's experience.'

21

The *Midvale Chronicle* had devoted most of its front page to the murder of Paula Mason. Under banner headlines it detailed what Maudie and everybody already knew, namely that the victim's body had been discovered by Scouts out on manoeuvres. However, on reading down the page she saw an interesting piece of information beneath a sub-heading that said, 'Note found. What appears to be a suicide note written by the victim in impeccable typing was pushed through the letterbox at our offices this week. The text of the missive is as follows:

'My darling Lenny. I cannot go on like this. If only you could understand the suffering you have caused me, you would not continue to reject me in this way. I have loved you since I first set eyes on you back there on Wellstead Common and I have never looked at another man. You led me to believe that you felt the same about me and that we would be married as soon as you were settled in your career. After everything we have been to each other, I cannot believe that you would fall out of love unless someone has been poisoning your mind against me. Please, please tell me that you will come back to me, or I shall be forced to take drastic steps. Yours eternally, your Paula.'

'It's a bit melodramatic, isn't it?' Mrs Hatch had been reading the story with her forefinger, following the lines of type. Maudie and two other women who had just purchased their papers had also read it.

'Melodramatic!' Maudie said. 'Somebody has been seeing too many tearjerker movies, I'd say.'

'Oh, but it calls it a suicide note, Nurse!' Mrs Frost exclaimed. 'That means it was written by that poor girl, doesn't it?'

'That's as may be, but Paula Mason didn't take her own life, Mrs Frost. Not unless she managed to whack herself over the head! And even supposing she did, where is the weapon she did it with? As far as I know, the police haven't found that yet.'

'Pills, Nurse. See, she takes sleeping pills. Then she goes to that hut and she comes over all dizzy and falls down, hitting her head on summat.' Mrs Frost nodded triumphantly.

'That's all very well,' Maudie pointed out, 'but how did this so-called letter get into the newspaper office?'

'Why, through the letterbox, of course. It says so right here.'

'That's not what I meant. If Miss Mason did commit suicide, how did she manage to deliver her note after she was dead? And why send them the letter — or a copy of it — that she had written to Dr Lennox? If she meant to expose him to ridicule or worse, why not write directly to the editor, stating her case?'

'Oh, well, the police will sort that out, I expect,' Mrs Hatch said, 'but look, there's more. Exclusive interview with victim's friend, see page three. 'Paula was so much in love with Lenny. It was like a fairy story.''

'I'll read it at home,' Maudie said. 'I expect it's only tripe, anyway.'

Little Mrs Frost sounded shocked. 'Oh,

no, Nurse! It must be true if it's in the newspaper.'

'And I'm the Archbishop of Canterbury!' Maudie told her as she marched out of the door.

★　★　★

Sitting on her sofa with her feet up and a cup of tea at her elbow, Maudie found that to her way of thinking the story was indeed rubbish. Still, it was certain to appeal to most of the *Chronicle*'s readers who, quite naturally, wanted to learn more about the murder that had taken place in their own district.

The interviewee, who had been tracked down by an enterprising reporter, was one Natalie Smith, 26, of Welstead, Berks. 'Poor little Paula was so beautiful and good,' Miss Smith was supposed to have said. 'I break down and cry every time I remember what has happened to her, and I hope that evil brute gets what's coming to him.'

'Asked if she believed that Paula's doctor boyfriend was the killer, Miss

Smith told our reporter that she wouldn't like to say. 'I always try to think the best of people until it's proved otherwise,' the pretty redhead insisted.'

'I should jolly well think so, too,' Maudie muttered. 'The stupid girl must know she'd be leaving herself open to a lawsuit if she said otherwise. What a lot of codswallop!'

Still, Maudie was interested to learn more about Paula's background. Until now she had been something of a mystery woman. The story was ordinary enough. She had come from a modest home, leaving the local council school at fifteen. Her parents had managed to scrape together the fees charged by a business college, where Paula went to learn typing, shorthand and rudimentary book-keeping skills. Natalie Smith had been a fellow student there.

'We both landed good jobs in the typing pool at Marston's, the clothing factory,' Natalie had gone on to say. 'Paula was very ambitious, always talking about how she was going to better herself, how she meant to become a somebody. I expected her to move on after a while, possibly to get a job as a private secretary to some prominent businessman, but she stayed with us, year after year. We were always friends. As it happened, we celebrated out twenty-first birthdays together.'

'Asked how it was that the victim had come to know Dr Lennox, Miss Smith said that she could certainly tell us about that. 'A group of us used to go about together all the time, you know the kind of thing. We went to the pictures every week and we attended the Saturday night hops down the youth club. Then we started going to the baths to swim, and that's when we met Lenny. Most of the time he was away at some posh boarding school, but we used to see him during the holidays. He told us he was captain of his school swimming team and he had to practise, to keep in shape. Well, Paula was a good swimmer and they used to race up and down the pool, seeing who could beat the other.'

Maudie read on, learning that the holiday friendships had continued over the years. Leonard Lennox had gone off to university and then entered medical school. Determined to impress him, Paula had learned to play tennis and joined the local tennis club, where his parents were members. She had studied books of etiquette and another on 'how to dress for success'. She had learned to use makeup skillfully, and had saved up to get a hairdo in a fashionable salon.

In other words, thought Maudie, she was setting her cap at Lenny Lennox. Her efforts seemed to have worked, for the young medical student occasionally asked her out on dates during his infrequent visits home.

* * *

'Of course Paula understood that there was no question of marriage until he qualified as a doctor,' Natalie went on, 'but she was prepared to wait. She had plenty of other chances, but Lenny was her one true love. I don't know what went wrong between them, but whatever it was it can never be put right now, with poor Paula cold in her grave. It is such a terrible tragedy.'

Maudie crumpled the paper in disgust. 'Crass sensationalism!' she muttered. Stripped of its emotional embellishments, the story was common enough. Two young people come together for a while, but in time one of them moves on, leaving the other bereft and disappointed. Perhaps Paula had hoped to marry the man of her dreams, although whether it was from love or mere ambition nobody but the girl herself could know for sure.

It could be, too, that the young medical student had led her on with false promises; or perhaps he had meant what he said at the time, before outgrowing the relationship. Paula had come to Llandyfan insisting that she was engaged to marry Dr Lennox; he had sworn to Maude that this was a figment of the girl's imagination. What was the truth of the matter? The only person who now knew what had happened was Dr Lennox himself, and considering the predicament he was in he was not about to say otherwise.

Maudie reached for the scissors. As a police officer, Dick would be interested in this story, and she wanted to send him the clipping when she wrote to him. Even if it cost a lot to enclose it in an airmail envelope, it would be worth it, for she had very little news that would interest him apart from this murder.

Dick Bryant tended to get a bit squeamish when gynaecological details were brought up, so she couldn't say much about her life on the job. Heaven help him if he ever had to deliver a baby, as occasionally police officers did in an emergency. And people said that females were the weaker sex!

22

'I've got a terrible headache, Nurse. It's come on all of a sudden, and I feel sick with it. Am I having a stroke?' Rita Grayson looked at Maudie with panic in her eyes.

'Is your vision blurred?' Maudie asked, hunting in Dr Lennox's desk drawer for a small torch, which she shone in her patient's eyes. 'Is your nose bunged up? Is there any severe throbbing pain in your forehead? You haven't bumped your head recently?'

Maudie was fairly sure that sinusitis and more serious conditions could be ruled out, and the woman confirmed that she was not a sufferer from migraines. She knew that Mrs Grayson was under great stress, trying to hold down a job at the button factory while catering to her unemployed husband and four boys at home. That was enough to give anybody a headache.

'Is everything all right at work, Mrs Grayson?'

'It's no worse than usual, I suppose. It gets me down sometimes, standing in that production line day in, day out, but at least it pays. And don't you tell me I have to stay off work for a rest, Nurse, because if I lose my job we'll be in a right pickle.'

'Your hubby still hasn't found work?'

'Are you kidding? The day that man starts looking will be the day the sun rises in the evening. Work-shy, that's his trouble I reckon.'

'Is there something else that's making you feel anxious?'

Mrs Grayson stifled a sob. 'You haven't heard, then? The results of the eleven plus are out, and our Johnny failed.'

'Ah.' Maudie gave her a sympathetic smile. 'I'm sorry to hear that. I know how badly you wanted to send him to the grammar school.'

'It's my belief they failed him on account of what he did. You know, throwing that brick through the Nevilles' widow. I knew that would happen. I just knew it!'

'I don't think it works that way,' Maudie murmured.

'Anyway, my hubby's no help. He says it's just as well he failed, because the sooner our John finishes school the sooner he can go out to work and earn his keep. And we couldn't have afforded to kit him out in that fancy uniform, the blazer and all that. Dot Neville showed me the list for the girls' school and it's as long as your arm. The boys' grammar wouldn't be no better.'

'Ah!' Maudie said. 'So her girls passed the scholarship, then?'

'Well no, that's the thing. Hazel got in but not Holly.'

'My goodness! That's going to be a bit awkward.'

The Neville girls were twins, who had never been separated in their lives. Now they were due to undergo a painful parting of the ways. One child would go off to the grammar school at Midvale, dressed in its distinctive uniform, and she would study various subjects geared towards leaving school with good qualifications. If she was successful academically she might even go on to become a nurse or a teacher.

Her sister would go to the other school, known as the secondary modern, which would provide her with a general education until she left school at fifteen. If she did well here she could still make a success of her life, although many schoolgirls were only biding their time until marriage and motherhood claimed them.

Sadly, there was a social gap between pupils at the two schools. The girls at the secondary modern regarded their grammar school counterparts as snobs, and their taunts could be heard on the streets at home time. For their part, the girls at 'the grammar' looked down on their foes with disdain.

Schooldays are supposed to be the happiest days of your life, but they are full of such petty annoyances. And this would surely drive a wedge between the sisters. Maudie said as much to Rita Grayson.

'Dot knows that. She says she won't let Hazel go to the grammar. It's not fair on their Holly.'

'Oh, I say! What about poor Hazel?

This could affect her whole life.'

'She's going to let them both do another year at the village school. Miss Rice thinks the twins will be allowed to have a second go at the scholarship. At least, Holly will. So perhaps it'll all work out in the end.'

Maudie sighed. 'Oh well, it's their business, I suppose. Now then, you're to take a couple of Aspro every four hours, and you simply must get some rest, Mrs Grayson. Put your feet up with a nice book and leave all your worries behind you.'

'Fat chance!' the patient said, getting up to leave. 'No rest for the wicked, Nurse, and I reckon I must have been really bad in a past life to get landed with my load now.' She laughed mirthlessly and left the room.

* * *

When Maudie returned to her cottage she was thrilled to find a long-awaited letter from Dick lying on the doormat. She hoped it was a newsy missive, and not one of the juvenile 'How are you? I am well' variety that she had sometimes read out to sick patients in hospital.

She discovered that it was all about Toronto, where Dick had spent his first few days on Canadian soil. He informed her that it was set on the shores of Lake Ontario which, as she recalled from her school geography lessons, was one of the Great Lakes. Apparently the city had a cathedral, universities, and a number of boarding schools that were modelled on the English public school system.

'Except that what they call a public school here is actually the sort of council school we are used to. Actually I'm having a bit of trouble with the language. What we know as scones they call biscuits, and if you really do want a biscuit you have to ask for cookies. As for baps, they've never heard of such a thing. And I thought they spoke English in Canada!

'This week I'm being sent out to a rural area and assigned to a partner. You'll never believe this, Maudie, but I'm being given a handgun! The police here are armed, even in places where trouble rarely seems to happen. I told one of the chaps here that I've only been used to a truncheon, and he couldn't believe that either. 'Not much good when you're chasing rustlers,' he said. I'm not sure if he was joking!'

The letter broke off at that point, and started up again in a different shade of ink. 'Got to run. One of the chaps here has invited me to his home for a meal. It will be nice to see how ordinary people live here. Chin up, Maudie! Don't work too hard! Yours sincerely, Dick.'

'Sincerely!' Maudie spluttered. 'Is that all you can say, Dick Bryant? What happened to 'love'?'

She knew that he wasn't a demonstrative man, at least when it came to letting his feelings show; possibly that had something to do with his police training. But surely he could do a bit better on paper? When she replied she would be a bit more effusive, and that should give him a hint. She glanced at the top of the letter and saw, to her dismay, that he hadn't given her a return address. Perhaps that was because he was about to move to a new location and hadn't yet been told where he'd be staying.

Well, there was nothing to stop her replying. She would answer his letter and keep the pages in an envelope on the mantelpiece, ready to send off in due course.

'You've missed another murder!' she began. No, no — there was no need to sound so gleeful. Someone had died in horrible circumstances, and that had to be a cause for regret. One could only hope that death had come swiftly, catching the victim unawares, and that she didn't suffer. Maudie crumpled up the paper, tossed it in the direction of the waste-paper basket, and began again.

'Work is difficult at the moment. Dr Lennox has been arrested for murder and I'm having to take his surgery and take on some of his home visits.' This was another non-starter. It made it sound as if the poor man had indeed killed someone, which she trusted was not the case. Furthermore, it sounded as if she were moaning, or boasting, which was not the impression she wished to convey. Another ball of paper flew through the air and landed on the carpet.

The doorbell rang, and with a cry of annoyance she struggled to her feet and went to see who wanted her. There was nobody in sight. Muttering, she closed the door and returned to her letter. The bell rang a second time. Again there was nobody outside, but she thought she could hear muffled giggling around the corner. Now she knew what was going on; it was children playing what they called rat-tat ginger.

'Right, then! We'll put a stop to this!' she said grimly. Standing behind the door, clutching a jug full of cold water, she waited for the bell to ring again. When it did she flung the door open and hurled the contents of her jug into the air. 'Take that, you little monkeys!' she shouted, pasting an evil smile on her face. That would teach them!

Her grin faded abruptly when she realised what she had done. Dr Dean stood on her doorstep, his hair dripping and his smart suit drenched with water.

23

'Oh, Dr Dean! I'm so sorry! Oh, I do apologise! There were children, you see. Do come in, please. I'll fetch a towel.' Maudie knew she was babbling, but the self-important Dr Dean was the last person she wished to offend.

'Is this how you treat all your guests?' he enquired, looking down his long nose at the towel she handed him before beginning to dab at his garments with a look of distaste on his face. Dr Lennox might have said the same thing in similar circumstances, she knew, but she felt sure that he'd have laughed it off. After all, apart from the initial shock, there was no harm in a bit of clean water, was there?

'Won't you sit down, Dr Dean? Can I offer you a cup of coffee? It's only Camp, I'm afraid, but the milk was delivered fresh this morning.'

'I don't care for coffee essence, Nurse. Chicory is not to my taste.'

'Tea, then?'

'This is not a social visit, Nurse.'

'I see.' Maudie waited.

The doctor began to pace around the room, still dabbing at his damp trousers. 'I have been to the Beasley estate to see Mr Munroe,' he said.

'Oh, yes? I didn't know that he was unwell. Of course this whole business of his cousin is most distressing for him.'

'As far as I know the man is in perfect health. And he appears to be taking Lennox's trouble in his stride. His problem is with you, Nurse Rouse.'

'Me?' Maudie stared at Dr Dean over the top of her reading glasses.

'Yes. He has laid a complaint against you, asserting that you are insolent, undisciplined and incompetent, and he wants you removed. Having listened to him I believe that he has a point, but I told him that in all fairness I had to speak to you first, to see if you have any explanation to offer. That is why I am here.'

Flabbergasted, Maudie sank down on the chair she had vacated in order to answer the door. 'I don't know what to say, Dr Dean. Perhaps if you tell me what it is I'm accused of, I'll be better equipped to respond. And do sit down. I can't think straight with you looming over me like that.' For a moment she thought she'd gone too far, giving another example of what Bingo would call insolence, but Dr Dean sat down at the table without comment.

'I admit that Mr Munroe and I haven't always seen eye to eye,' Maudie said, wishing she hadn't used that word 'admit', which made her words seem like a confession. 'But if anyone has done something out of place, it's him.'

'Mr Munroe tells me that Lennox left him in full charge during his absence, Nurse.'

'Perhaps in a small way; opening up the surgery in the morning, making a note of incoming calls, and so on. Beyond that there isn't a lot he can do. He has absolutely no medical experience, Dr Dean. He hasn't even taken first-aid training with the St John Ambulance, as some our villagers have. I've caught him snooping through patients' records, even advising some of them how to deal with any minor complaints they may have brought to us.'

'He more or less says the same about you, Nurse. 'She's not competent to take surgery,' he says. 'She's only a midwife, not even a real nurse.' Those were his very words.' Maudie stared at Dr Dean. Surely he didn't go along with this twaddle? He knew better.

Of course she was a real nurse, and a highly qualified one, too! As for being 'only a midwife', well, nurses had to gain their state registration before they went on to take their midwifery training. Was it possible that Bingo equated her with the sort of village women who attended confinements having no training at all except for having observed others of their kind in action? Things had been done in this way throughout the centuries and many of these old wives were competent enough, and the mothers they served had good reason to thank them for their ministrations. Then, too, the mortality rate for mother and child had been far too high, with postpartum complications often taking their toll.

Maudie gave herself a mental shake. This was no time to be dwelling on the social implications of the midwife in the field! 'Well, Doctor, I'm sorry that Mr Munroe feels this way. As he says, I am only a midwife, and since I've been found wanting I suppose I won't be required to man the surgery any longer. What will happen now? Will you bring in a locum for the duration? Or will you deal with it all yourself? People will expect me to know.'

Dr Dean frowned. With low cunning, Maudie went in for the kill. 'If I might make a suggestion, Doctor, why don't you change the surgery hours until later in the day? You could see your Midvale patients in the morning, make your house calls right after lunch, and then see Dr Lennox's patients in the late afternoon or evening' She paused. 'With any luck you won't get hauled out of bed too many nights in a row to deal with emergencies.'

He glared at her. 'All right, Nurse, you've made your point. This is far too much for one man. We'll have to come to some sort of accommodation between us.'

Maudie smothered a grin and waited. Prior to the coming of the National Health Service, old Doc Mallory had kept far more patients on his list than Dr Dean was contemplating now. He had done the job with the help of dedicated women who were 'only' nurses!

'Don't you think you could patch things up with Mr Munroe, Nurse? The man is only trying to keep things humming over until Lennox returns. That's if he ever does.'

'I'm prepared to try, but only if our respective duties are clearly outlined and understood, Dr Dean. I'm afraid that in his zeal to reduce the number of patients waiting to be seen, Mr Munroe is inclined to ask people what's the matter with them, and if the answer is something minor — a rash, let's say, or a troublesome cough — he tells them about some ancient remedy his granny used to use, and suggests they go back home and try it. The problem is that because he's the doctor's cousin, work-ing in the surgery, people assume he must have some official standing. Nine times out of ten these old folk remedies do no harm, but what about the rest of the time? And who has to shoulder the blame when things go wrong? We could have a lawsuit on our hands, Dr Dean. You or I could be struck off the register, and Dr Lennox along with us. In fact, I'm not so sure where we stand right now. If anyone decided to complain about all this to the General Medical Council, we could be in real trouble.'

At least, you could, Doctor, she thought. *I've protested against old Bingo being there, so I'm in the clear. So what are you going to do next, then?*

'I had no idea about all this, Nurse,' Dr Dean said. His face had turned white at the implications of what Maudie had relayed to him. 'I shall have words to say to our Mr Munroe. At the same time, Nurse, I trust you are not exceeding your authority?'

'Oh, no, Doctor,' Maudie said meekly. 'Of course I refer all the serious cases to you. But I am a nurse and of course I feel qualified to prescribe certain treatments in minor cases, dishing out mag sulph, soda bic, and so on.' She had used medical jargon for epsom salts and bicarbonate of soda. 'If I passed on all those cases to you, there would be no point in opening the surgery at the gatehouse, would there? They might as well all go to see you at Midvale in the first place.'

'Quite so. Quite so.'

'So where does this leave me, Dr Dean?'

'I shall speak to the man, of course, and make it clear to him that he is not permitted to question the patients in any way, and he is certainly not to suggest how their ailments might be treated. But if he agrees to those conditions he may stay on. Surely he'll be needed to announce the patients to you?'

'Oh, but Mr Munroe is a newcomer, whereas I've lived here for years and I can put a name to every face.' *And the same can't be said for you, Dr Dean,* she thought. 'And I've brought a good many of their children into this world,' she went on. 'Mr Munroe will have to ask their names before ushering them in to announce them to the nurse they know well. People are going to find that pretty strange. A waste of time, I'd call it.'

'Well, if you really think you can manage . . . '

'Yes, thank you, Doctor.' Maudie felt like telling him that she had managed very well here, during and after the war, and she had never flagged in her efforts to give the people of her district the best possible care she could offer. Best not to gild the lily, though, she told herself.

'Very well, then, you may carry on as before, and we'll see how you do, Nurse. I'll speak to Mr Munroe and tell him he's to keep his nose out of surgery matters, although that will be awkward, given the fact that he's one of the family. Are you sure you can't come to some sort of truce with him, Nurse?'

'No, Dr Dean.'

'So be it, then.' Game, set and match to Maudie Rouse!

* * *

Dr Dean left at last, and when he had gone she waltzed around her little living room, rejoicing in her victory. She stopped suddenly, seeing in her mind's eye a vision of her own deceased granny. That lady had been fond of quoting from the Bible, and now she seemed to be warning Maudie: pride goeth before destruction, and a haughty sprit before a fall. Proverbs 16, verse 18.

'I'd better watch it,' Maudie decided.

24

Rita Grayson put her head around the door of Maudie's office in the parish hall. 'There you are, Nurse. I'm glad I caught you before you went up to the surgery. The fact is, we've had a bit of good news and I wanted to share it with you.'

'Oh, yes?'

'It's Johnny, Nurse. He's in!'

'In? In where?'

'He's got into the grammar, of course! Dot Neville has decided to keep their Hazel back, so now my little lad can take her place. Isn't it absolutely marvellous?'

'Oh, Mrs Grayson,' Maudie said, hating to destroy the woman's happiness, 'are you sure? I don't think it works that way. If Hazel can't take up her scholarship I'm sure that can't affect the boys' school.'

'But that's what I'm trying to tell you, Nurse! It appears that our John only failed by a whisker, and now this place is

212

on offer it will go to him. We've had a letter from them saying he's to start in September! I'm so proud I could burst!'

'Then I'm delighted for you,' Maudie told her. 'What does Johnny think?'

'All that boy cares about is football, but I suppose he's pleased. We promised him a new pair of football boots if he passed, so he's looking forward to getting those. Mind you, we'll have to dig deep into our pockets to pay for the uniform. The blazer alone costs near a week's wages. I've told our Stan he'll have to buckle to and do a hand's turn for once. No more drinking in the Royal Oak, even if we can manage to pay for the boy's clothes on the Never-Never.'

This, Maudie knew, was a system of credit where people could purchase goods by paying in instalments, at so much a week. It derived its name from the fact that, with interest tacked on, the buyer was never finished paying for the items in question.

Maudie could see the flaws in this scheme. People were likely to get carried away, buying more than they could afford. If they defaulted on their payments partway through, their goods would be repossessed, leaving them with nothing to show for their trouble. Maudie preferred the old-fashioned method, where you placed a deposit on the item you wanted and paid so much a week until you were able to carry it home in triumph. Still, such a method wouldn't help Johnny Grayson. If he were to start at the grammar school in September, he would have to be properly kitted out.

★   ★   ★

There was a sequel to this piece of news. Len Frost, the landlord of the Royal Oak, turned up at the surgery complaining of piles. 'At least, there's this lump . . . ' he told Maudie, in an offhand tone. She knew what was worrying him, of course. Whenever patients came across a lump of any description they immediately suspected cancer, which was only natural, even though nine times out of ten the trouble was caused by something benign.

Having examined him and found a haemorrhoid the size of a garden pea protruding from the anus, Maudie explained that this was the result of a swollen vein, or in layman's terms, piles. 'The chemist will give you some special suppositories,' she advised him, 'and you must eat a high-fibre diet, including plenty of fruit and vegetables. You don't want to get con-stipated, Mr Frost, because it's straining during lavatory visits that has caused this trouble. There are other things the doctor can do to help, but let's try this first, shall we? And if you start passing blood you must consult the doctor right away. Although that might happen with piles, it can also be a sign of something more.'

'Right-ho, Nurse,' he said, pulling up his trousers. 'Did you get a look at Stan Grayson this morning?'

'No, he hasn't been in. Why do you say that? Has he had an accident?'

The landlord grinned. 'Not to say an accident, Nurse. More like a collision, see. The shiner he's got make him looks like he's done ten rounds with Joe Louis, and lost.'

'I'll pop in on my way home and take a look at him,' Maudie promised. 'Tell the next patient to come in on your way out, will you, Mr Frost?'

True to her word, she stopped at the Graysons' home, but nobody answered the door. Rita would be at her work in Midvale, of course, and the boys would be at school. The baby would be with his granny. The father of the family would most likely be in the pub, drowning his sorrows, but if that was where he was he could jolly well stay there. She had better things to do than run round after drunken sots.

A distant clatter of ironmongery alerted her to the fact that someone was out back, unless of course a dog was rooting through the dustbin. Maudie made her way around the side of the house, trying to avoid broken toys and what looked like bicycle parts that were strewn all over the pathway. Decent stockings were hard enough to come by without sacrificing them to a patient's trash.

A man dressed in moleskin trousers and a collarless shirt was hurling broken china into a bucket. 'Mr Grayson?' Maudie asked, for although she had brought several of his sons into the world she had never met the man before. In common with many expectant fathers, he tended to retreat to the pub until the drama was over. She liked to think that most men went to drown their sorrows in the company of others because they feared for their wives' safety, but she had her doubts about this chap.

'Who wants to know?' He continued his task without looking in her direction. She took his words to mean that he was indeed Rita Grayson's unemployed husband.

'I'm Nurse Rouse.'

'The wife's at work. We don't want no midwife, and you'd better not bring no more kids here because we've got too many in this house as it is!'

Maudie scratched her forehead. Did the fool think she waved her magic wand and his wife miraculously became pregnant? She refused to follow that thought.

That way lay madness!

'I understand you've had an accident, Mr Grayson. I've come to look at your eye.'

'Get lost!' he shouted, holding up his head for the first time. Maudie gasped. Len Frost was right — the chap was certainly sporting a ghastly black eye.

'How on earth did you come by that bruise, Mr Grayson?'

'If you must know, the wife whacked me with the frying pan! And then she took a fit and started throwing plates around. I'm a battered husband, ain't I? But you keep that to yourself, missy. I don't want folks saying I'm a ninny that can't stand up for myself!'

'My goodness!'

'And now you're here you can tell me what you're going to do about this eye of mine. I've heard tell a raw beefsteak is just the thing to slap on it. You don't happen to have one on you, do you?'

'You'd be lucky. It's years since I've tasted steak, and if I had one now I certainly wouldn't waste it on your black eye. I suggest you wring out a cloth in cold water and hold that to your eye. Good day to you, Mr Grayson.'

Maudie went on her way, feeling puzzled. She had met a few violent husbands in her time, but this was something new. Could it be true? She made up her mind to meet the Midvale bus when the factory workers were coming home, and have a word with Rita Grayson. She didn't seem like a violent person, but that didn't mean much. While doing her time in the casualty ward at her training hospital in the big city, Maudie had patched up many a victim of domestic abuse. If there was one thing she had learned it was that outsiders could never know what went on behind closed doors. A man — or woman — who presented a perfectly reasonable face to the world might be a cruel despot when nobody was near to observe what was going on.

Time and again, Maudie had heard it said that nobody should interfere between partners in a marriage for fear of making matters worse, but she didn't hold with that. If in her capacity as a nurse she could gently read the riot act, it might be all that was needed to break the wall of silence. If there was violence in the Grayson home, there were children to think of.

25

'Have you heard the latest, Nurse?' Mrs Blunt seemed so distressed that Maudie could not imagine what had happened. Had the church roof fallen in? The parishioners had been trying to raise the money for repairs but so far their efforts had been in vain. The vicar's wife didn't wait for a response and went on with her tale of woe.

'Cora Beasley has confessed to the murder of Paula Mason!'

'Oh, come on, Mrs Blunt. That's not one bit funny.'

'But it's true, Nurse. It was on the wireless this morning.'

'It can't be. I was at the surgery and so was Bingo Munroe. He didn't say a word.'

'Perhaps he didn't know.'

'The news hounds must have got it wrong.'

Mrs Blunt shook her head sadly. 'I'm

afraid not. Harold received a call from the police station. Her family solicitor is out of town and Mrs Beasley is in such a state that the police felt she should have someone with her to bolster her up. It seems that she walked into the police station this morning and insisted that they let Dr Lennox go because she was the real culprit.'

'Good grief!'

'What are you two gossiping about?' a stern voice asked.

Maudie and Mrs Blunt looked up guiltily. 'Harold! There you are, dear. And we were not gossiping. I felt that Nurse should be told the facts because she may be called upon to offer comfort, or medical assistance.'

'To whom?'

'How do I know? Mr Munroe, perhaps. Don't be cross, Harold. It's our duty to comfort the afflicted, as you very well know!'

The vicar grunted. 'As far as I can see the only affliction is in Mrs Beasley's mind. Can you imagine her bludgeoning someone to death? And she the president of the Mothers' Union! If you ask me, she's having a brainstorm brought on by the shock and disgrace of the murder, and the part her nephew allegedly played in it.'

'Did she say why she did it?' Maudie asked. 'All right, all right; I agree with you, Vicar. She seems an unlikely murderess. But given that she did confess to the crime, she must have given a reason.'

'She says she did it on the spur of the moment. She didn't like Paula Mason and thought of her as a most unsuitable bride for Dr Lennox. 'Simply not one of us,' that's what she told me. She tried to reason with the girl — even offered her a substantial amount of money to go away and leave him alone — but Paula only laughed at her. Mrs Beasley lost her temper, picked up the murder weapon, and attacked Paula as she turned to leave.'

'And what was the weapon?' Maudie asked with interest.

'I'm afraid she wasn't too clear on that point. Whatever it was happened to be lying about in the hut — a bit of old farm machinery, perhaps — and that is what she used.'

'And what did she do with the weapon after she left Paula for dead?'

'Naturally the police asked her that. At first she said she'd thrown it into the duck pond, but on being told that the pond would be dragged in order to locate the weapon, to be used as evidence in court, she changed her mind and said she was so horrified by what she'd done she could no longer remember.'

'The old amnesia alibi. Very convenient,' Maudie muttered.

'That's not very charitable, Nurse.'

'Phooey. I don't believe a word of this. Do you?'

'I admit I find it hard to believe,' the vicar said slowly, 'but on the other hand I'm sure that Mrs Beasley would not lie.'

'Be that as it may, it must be one thing or the other, Mr Blunt. It seems to me that she's doing a Sydney Carton act, sacrificing herself to protect her nephew by confessing to a crime she did not commit. And that is very foolish of her, in more ways than one.'

'I don't quite understand,' Mrs Blunt murmured.

'Don't you see? The police are no more going to believe she's capable of murder than you are. A gentlewoman in her seventies, a pillar of the church; is it likely? By confessing she'll leave the police with the impression that she thinks — no, that she's sure — that Dr Lennox is guilty. I'm sure she meant well, but she's only made things worse. She'll be jolly lucky if they don't charge her with wasting police time.'

* * *

Maudie paced up and down, waiting for the Midvale bus to arrive. Rita Grayson clambered down, clutching a string bag that held a variety of tinned goods. She must have gone shopping during her lunch hour, Maudie surmised. The woman smiled when she saw Maudie.

'Hello, Nurse. Waiting for the bus, were you?'

'No, Mrs Grayson. I was waiting for

you, actually. Can I have a word?'

'Can it wait, Nurse? I can't stop now; I have to go to Mum's to fetch the baby.'

'This won't take long. I'll walk along with you, if I may.'

'I think I know what this is about,' Rita sighed, falling into step behind Maudie. 'You've seen our Stan, haven't you?'

'That's right, and I wondered . . . '

'You wondered if it was me who'd given him a bashing. Well, you're right! I flew off the handle and I bopped him one with the frying pan. Then I threw a few plates across the room, just to relieve the tension, like. Oh, Nurse, I've never done such a thing before and I hope I never will again, but he made me so mad! I had the pan in my hand, just about to do him a fry-up, and when he said what he did one thing just led to another.'

'And what was it he said?'

'I'd been saying how we had to do things different now the boy is going to the grammar. Stan would have to give up swilling beer down the Royal Oak, and he'd need to find a job that brought in more money than the dole. There's labouring work to be had on the building sites, and there's fieldwork for them as isn't too proud to do it.

'Well, Nurse, he said there was no need for our John to go to that posh school. The council school had been good enough for him and his father before him. He could read and write and reckon; what more does a man need? He told me I was getting above myself, with a lot of foolish notions.'

'I can see how that might annoy you, Mrs Grayson.'

'Annoy me! I should jolly well think it did! Me, getting above myself? I can tell you, when I heard that, everything came bubbling up and boiled over. Here's me going out to work to support us all, while he idles his life away. And what do I come home to? All the housework, and the kids, and him saying he wants his rights in the bedroom. And half the time I'm slaving over the wash when everyone else is fast asleep, running sheets through the mangle and then struggling out to the clothesline in the dark. I've had it, Nurse! The worm has turned!'

26

Maudie was thrilled to find a letter from Dick awaiting her when she reached home. It seemed to be ages since she had heard from him. He had written to say that he was now billeted in a small town near Ottawa, helping to maintain law and order in the surrounding rural area.

'I thought it was going to be like Midvale on a larger scale, but this has to be seen to be believed. Take the schools for instance. The countryside is dotted with these little buildings; one-roomed schoolhouses, they call them. Pupils of all ages and standards are taught by one teacher, usually a young woman not much older than themselves. The kiddies have to walk to school — no buses out in the country — and I can't imagine what that's like in winter. According to my opposite number there are times when they have several feet of snow on the ground, although I'm not sure if he's pulling my leg!

'The people here are very friendly and welcoming, just as long as newcomers don't criticise what they find. I met one chap the other day who was fresh out from London, and he was complaining about the plumbing out on the farms, which usually consists of a well and a good old-fashioned privy. The ladies he was speaking to listened to this until they could get a word in edgewise, and then one looked him straight in the eye and said, 'Well, if the Old Country is so wonderful, why don't you go back there, then?' That took the wind out of his sails, I can tell you.'

Maudie sighed. She was interested in Dick's doings, of course she was, but his letters never included anything personal. Didn't he miss her? She peered inside the envelope to see if he had enclosed any-thing else; once before he had included a clipping from a local newspaper that had mentioned Dick and his arrival in the district: 'British Bobby Finds New Beat'.

There was a snapshot there. She had never seen a colour snap before, only black and white. Perhaps the technology hadn't reached Britain yet, but the Canadians, being so close to America where all sorts of luxuries were available, were probably quite used to it.

There was Dick, sitting at some sort of outdoor table, grinning away at the camera. And she could see why he was grinning, too. A young woman clad in a sleeveless green blouse and the briefest of white shorts was leaning over his shoulder, with her arms wrapped around him.

Maudie turned the picture over. Somebody had written on the back in what was definitely not Dick's handwriting: 'Corn boil Ruthie and Dick'.

Maudie looked at the photo again, glaring at Ruthie and Dick. Who was this blonde bombshell draped over Dick? And what on earth was a corn boil? Was it some sort of medical condition found only in Canada? If there was such a disease, she hoped that Ruthie had it. Hadn't anyone told her that Dick Bryant was practically a married man?

When Maudie turned back to the letter to see if there was any mention of this Ruthie, she was shocked to read the date at the top of the page, having skimmed over it earlier. Either this letter had been lost in the post, or he had forgotten to post it. And why hadn't he written since? They couldn't be making him work around the clock, so there was no excuse for him.

Annoyed, she began to pace around the room. 'Stop this, right now!' she said aloud. 'There could be a perfectly good explanation!'

'Such as?' the imp on her shoulder demanded.

'Such as, he saved this Ruthie from drowning just before she was about to be swept over a waterfall, and the girl was just expressing her gratitude.'

'Oh, yeah? And while he was performing the heroic deed he struck his hand on a rock, did he, and that's why he can't write?'

Maudie tried to laugh at herself. It was ridiculous to jump to conclusions like this. Was she actually jealous? She would wait for a few days before she answered Dick's letter, and then she would casually ask him what a corn boil was.

★　★　★

Daisy Larke's husband rapped on Maudie's door on his way to work. 'Our Daisy wants to know if you could make a house call, Nurse. Would you be good enough to drop in today? She's that worried she can't think straight.'

'Of course I will. Is she worried about her pregnancy? Do you know if she's passing blood?'

'Nothing like that, Nurse. It's our Richard. He's come out in a rash and she's afraid it's the German measles.'

'All right, Mr Larke. I'll pop in this morning.'

When he had gone on his way, whistling, Maudie hastily rearranged her schedule so she could call on Daisy before surgery hours. If she was a bit late, Bingo would just have to hold the fort.

Daisy was probably aware, though her husband apparently was not, that if a pregnant woman was exposed to the German measles virus the developing baby could be seriously affected. The likelihood of damage being done occurred in the first trimester of pregnancy and Daisy was already five months along, but even so nothing was certain. The sooner Daisy received reassurance, the better for all concerned.

Little Richard was grizzling in his cot when Maudie arrived. Although his curls were damp with moisture his temperature was normal, and the glands in his neck were not swollen. The red rash that Daisy pointed out was nothing like the pink spots that Maudie associated with German measles.

'What is it, Nurse? What's the matter with our Richard?'

'Heat rash, Daisy. We're having a hot day for once and you've got him all bundled up in a jumper and a woolly pilch. You've got a galvanised bathtub, haven't you?

'Yes, Nurse. It's hanging up in the coal shed.'

Maudie knew that the scullery had been converted into a room for Fred Miller, Daisy's old father who had come to live with them some months before. That accounted for the unusual storage place for the old bath.

'Right. We'll fill it with cool water and

put it outside in the shade. Then we'll pop Richard into it with his rubber duck, and he'll have the time of his life. Mind you, you'll have to keep your eye on him. Don't let him out of your sight for a minute. A toddler can drown in two inches of water, you know.'

Maudie sat in the kitchen, stripping little Richard down to his nappy while she waited for Daisy to return. If only all life's problems could be solved in such a simple and pleasurable way! Old Fred had been sitting in the inglenook and now he spoke up suddenly, making her jump.

'I want a word with you, Nurse. Quick now, and let me say my piece before our Daisy comes back. I can hear her at the pump, filling that thing, and I don't want her listening what I'm talking about.'

'Is your arthritis playing you up again, Mr Miller? I'm afraid we'll have to have you looked at in hospital if it gets much worse.'

'My aches and pains are not nearly so bad since that damp spell went away, but it's you I want to talk about. That chap of yours has fallen by the wayside, ain't he?

Oh, there's no need to give me that look, Nurse. Why else would you have a face on you that looks like a wet week in Wigan?'

'I thank you for your concern, Mr Miller,' Maudie growled, 'but I really don't think that is any of your business. My fiancé has gone overseas in connection with his work, and as I told you the last time you brought this up, we hope to be married later this year.'

'Hope is a fine thing if it ain't misplaced, missy. You oughta bet on a certainty!'

'Nothing in life is certain, Mr Miller.'

'There would be if you wed me!'

Maudie laughed. 'You really shouldn't joke like that, Mr Miller. Somebody might take you seriously some day, and then where would you be?'

'So who's joking? I'd making you an honest offer, Nurse. I'll make you a good husband, you'll see. When we're wed I'll move into that little cottage of yours and we'll be snug as bugs in a rug. I'll have you to look after me in me old age and I'd be able to get to the Royal Oak once in a while to see me pals.'

Good grief! I really think he means it! Maudie thought. She looked him straight in the eye. 'And what's in it for me?' she asked.

'Why, you wouldn't be an old maid no longer, Nurse! You'd be a respectable married woman then. People would look up to you, see? And you'd have somebody to talk to on those dark winter evenings instead of skulking round that old cottage, all alone.'

Maudie didn't know whether to laugh or to cry. However she had been brought up to be considerate of other people's feelings whenever possible, so she pasted a smile on her face and began the process of letting her elderly swain down lightly.

'I do appreciate the offer, Mr Miller, and I consider it an honour to have been asked, but the answer is no. I'm sorry, but I'm spoken for, and I've given my word to Dick Bryant. I won't go back on that.'

'You ain't wearing no ring,' Fred grumbled. 'If you was properly engaged you'd be wearing a ring.'

'I'm a midwife. I'm not supposed to wear jewellery on duty. In any case, this is my final word on the subject and that's that.'

'I suppose it was worth a try,' the old fellow muttered. Maudie was relieved when Daisy came back inside to fetch little Richard. She seemed not to notice the strained silence in the kitchen and bore her son away with a cheery goodbye.

In the lane some time later Maudie dismounted from her bicycle, her shoulders shaking. She threw back her head and laughed until she cried. Good old Fred! Ready and willing to save her from spinsterhood, was he? And people would look up to her then? She sincerely hoped that was already the case.

27

'Dear Dick,' Maudie wrote. 'You'll never believe this, but I've had a proposal of marriage! From old Fred Miller, no less! You may remember my mentioning him before; he's the widower father of one of my patients, Daisy Larke. I was there the other day, making a visit to see her little boy, when the old boy came right out with it. Of course I thought he was joking, but he assured me he's deadly serious. Well, if you fall for some Canadian beauty and decide to throw me over, I'll be all set, ha, ha! No chance of my being left on the shelf now.'

There! That should set the cat among the pigeons. Dick might have a chuckle over this. He was unlikely to take Mr Miller's proposal as a threat, but it was his cue to give Maudie the response she hoped for. He could tell her that with her looks and delightful personality it was no wonder that other men wanted to sweep her off her feet, but she must remember that Dick Bryant was the one and only man for her. And pigs might fly! It might bring the Ruthie business to a head, though, causing him to think twice about continuing his dalliance with the girl, if indeed there was anything to it. Time to change the subject; no need to labour the point.

'I expect you'll be interested to know the latest about the murder. In all these weeks the police don't seem to have made any progress with the case. We've heard nothing more about that so-called suicide note; if the police have any thoughts on that subject they're not sharing them with the public. But there has been a development: Mrs Beasley has confessed to the killing! Of course nobody believes she could have done it, but I don't know where this leaves her, or Dr Lennox.'

Maudie threw down her pen. What more was there to say? If he commented on this at all, Dick would probably say that the woman should be charged with wasting police time. Or he might suggest that Mrs Beasley was an elderly woman;

could her wits be wandering? Senility was a sad thing when it overtook people who had been perfectly sensible all their lives.

Maudie's thoughts went to Stan Grayson's black eye. His wife was a decent woman, trying to do her best for her family under difficult circumstances. Suddenly driven too far, she had lashed out and hit her husband, whose behaviour was the root cause of her despair and frustration. Now she was sorry and ashamed. Fortunately no lasting harm had been done, in the physical sense at least.

The case of Paula Mason was different, but had her death been brought about by accident or design? Maudie considered the suspects: Dr Lennox; his aunt, Cora Beasley; his cousin, Bingo Munroe; and a person or persons unknown, call them X.

Dr Lennox first, because the police certainly seemed to believe in his guilt. He might have been driven to plan Paula's death, because he stood to lose so much by her continuing threats. Or he might equally have killed her on the spur of the moment being, like Rita Grayson, driven over the edge.

Cora Beasley. According to the vicar, she hadn't approved of the girl as a possible wife for her nephew. But no, Maudie couldn't see the old lady planning a cold-blooded murder. She, too, might have been driven to violence, and indeed she had confessed to such an act, but her story was too confused to ring true. Possibly the old girl was exhibiting signs of early senility.

Bingo Munroe. Well, there was no love lost between him and Maudie, but that was no reason to suspect him of murder. But he had wanted Paula for himself, and been spurned on more than one occasion. Had he approached her again and been turned down even more rudely? He, too, might have struck out in rage.

What about X? As usual, the villagers were pinning their hopes on the killer being an outsider — a passing tramp, say, or an opportunist who had killed her for whatever she might have in her handbag. It was known that she'd been staying at the Royal Oak and, modest though the accommodations there might be, they still cost money. She must have a bob or two about her.

What if the killer was someone from Paula's more recent past? Someone who held a grudge against her — for a reason Maudie couldn't fathom — and had followed her to Llandyfan? But no strangers had been observed in the neighbourhood, and it was one of those places where you couldn't so much as sneeze without everyone knowing about it.

Then there was the hut, deep in the woods on Mrs Beasley's land. What had Paula been doing there? Had the murderer lured her there, or had she asked somebody to meet her at that place? How had she even known about its existence?

Then there was the suicide letter. Who had delivered it to the newspaper, and how had they got hold of it in the first place? *Think, Maudie! Think!*

In the first place, it may not have been a genuine suicide note. Paula might have meant it as a tool to blackmail Dr Lennox with, having no intention of killing herself at all. But that wasn't the point. If she had sent it to him, what had become of it later? If he had left it lying about at home, it could only be someone under the same roof who had access to it. Bingo Munroe? Or the housekeeper, perhaps? Certainly not Cora Beasley.

Or, possibly, Lennox had thrust the note into his pocket and it had dropped out on the surgery floor, or even on the road outside. Someone had found it there and decided to use it against the doctor, but who could it be? Was it a public-spirited person, or a mischief-maker?

The words of a half-forgotten childhood game flashed through Maudie's mind.

I sent a letter to my love
And on the way I dropped it
One of you has picked it up
And put it in your pocket.

If you were the singer you then went around the circle of children, tapping each one on the shoulder: 'It wasn't you, it wasn't you, it wasn't you . . . ' Until at last you shouted, 'It was you!' And you ran like the wind with that person in hot pursuit, trying to get safely into her place in the circle before you were caught.

A dark shadow seemed to pass over Maudie, and she shuddered. This was not a game, and she would be wise to stay out of it. But when had Maudie Rouse ever stayed away from danger? She flirted with death every time she attended a woman in labour, knowing that sometimes it was only her skill and experience that brought mother and baby safely through their ordeal.

And she had a deeply ingrained sense of justice. If Dr Lennox was innocent of murder, then someone else was willing for him to take the rap, and possibly to pay the ultimate price at the end of the hangman's rope. That person must be found, and punished. He — or she — must not be allowed to get away with it. And if by chance Maudie was able to help to bring that about, well, it was her duty to do what she could. Even frail Mrs Beasley, misguided though her efforts were, had been willing to stand up for what she believed was right.

Maudie leapt up from the table, her letter to Dick forgotten. She left her cottage, carefully locking the door behind her. It was coming to something when you had to lock your doors in a place like Llandyfan, but there was a murderer out there somewhere and she had no wish to come home to find an intruder hiding behind the door.

Taking a short cut through the churchyard she shuddered again, remembering the time when she had done that in the dark and been accosted by an earlier killer. Had it not been for the intervention of a young couple who had been kissing and cuddling in the shade of an ancient yew tree, she might not have survived, although the man had later insisted that he was only trying to frighten her off.[1]

'You look as if you've seen a ghost, Nurse,' Mrs Blunt said when Maudie arrived at the back door of the rectory.

'Oh, I'm all right. Just a bit out of puff.

---

[1] *Blood Ties*

I think I'll have to lose a pound or two before Dick gets back. I've had too many cups of tea on my rounds, not to mention a bit of something to go with them.'

'I know what you mean,' Mrs Blunt said, patting her own ample girth. 'Now, what can I do for you, Nurse?'

28

'I want to see Mrs Beasley,' Maudie explained. 'I do hope she's not in custody?'

'Oh no,' Mrs Blunt said. 'They kept her hanging about for a few hours and then sent her home with a warning to behave herself in future. Harold thinks it was a disgraceful way to treat a woman of her advanced years, but in view of the circumstances I can't say I'm surprised.'

'So they didn't believe her confession, then.'

'Of course they didn't. To start with she's barely five-foot-two, and Miss Mason was very tall. When I first saw her I thought she might have been a mannequin, what with her looks and that height. How could Mrs Beasley have possibly swung her arm up high enough to hit the girl on the back of the head? I happen to know that she suffers arthritis in her neck and shoulders, too.'

'I wasn't aware of that.'

'No, you wouldn't be. I understand that Dr Mallory referred her to a specialist, well before your time, and she travels up to London once or twice a year to consult him. Not that there's much he can do, but I suppose it's a comfort to the poor soul.'

'I see. Well, there might be something I can do to make her more comfortable. She's back up at the house, then?'

Mrs Blunt looked at Maudie through narrowed eyes. 'You're not getting *involved*, are you, Nurse?'

Maudie's lips curved in a slight smile. 'I'm always involved with my patients. That's what my job is all about.'

'That's not what I meant, and you know that very well. You really must not go blundering about, placing yourself in harm's way.'

'I do not blunder,' Maudie said, her head held high. 'And where's the harm in visiting an elderly lady in her own home? What can she do to me, put poison in my teacup? Besides, I though we agreed that she's completely innocent of any wrong-doing?'

'I still don't like it. I know that Harold means to call on her this evening. Why not wait and go there with him? He'll give you a lift in his car.'

Maudie shook her head.

'Oh, all right, then. On your head be it. But before you do, there's something you should know. Dr Lennox has been transferred to the Martinsworth Facility.'

'The looney bin!' Maudie gasped.

'You mean the institution for the criminally insane,' Mrs Blunt corrected primly. 'And no, he isn't there as an inmate. They've had an outbreak of typhoid fever and the medical superintendent and several of his staff have gone down like ninepins, as well as an unspecified number of inmates. Dr Lennox volunteered to go there and see what he can do for the people there. I suppose it's the modern-day equivalent of going to work in a leper colony to atone for one's sins.'

'Phew!' Maudie said. 'I should have thought they'd have let him out on bail by now, since there's no proof he's actually done anything.'

'Apparently that was Mrs Beasley's

motive for going to see the police initially, but when she was told that wasn't possible in a case of murder she pulled out her trump card.'

'Her own confession. She must have had a fit when she found out he'd gone to Martinsworth to deal with an epidemic of typhoid, of all things. You hardly ever hear of that anymore, and certainly not in a hospital setting. I'm surprised that the police let him go there.'

'Perhaps they didn't know what else to do with him until the trial comes up. But he is a doctor, and if they are desperate for help I suppose he might as well be there making himself useful, instead of sitting in a cell somewhere.'

'And I had better make myself useful too,' Maudie decided, jumping up. 'I'm off to see Mrs Beasley, and if anyone comes looking for me, you'll know where to send them.'

'I do wish you'd wait for Harold,' Mrs Blunt murmured, but Maudie had gone. 'I might as well talk to the wall as try to convince Nurse Rouse when her mind is made up,' she told the cat. Perkin stared at her with wide-open green eyes, lifted his bushy tail and began to lick his bottom.

★   ★   ★

'She doesn't want to see anybody!' Bingo Munroe tried to slam the door in Maudie's face, but she planted her foot in the way and he was unable to dismiss her.

'I believe she'll see me,' Maudie said firmly.

'Then you're wrong! Kindly move along before I summon a policeman.'

'Who is it, Brian?' A weak voice was heard issuing from upstairs. 'Tell them to go away. I don't wish to speak to any more wretched reporters.'

'It's not a reporter, Mrs Beasley,' Maudie called, raising her voice so that the older woman would be able to hear her. 'It's Nurse Rouse. I've come to make sure you're quite well. May I come up?'

Without waiting for a reply, she pushed her way into the panelled hall and began to climb the stairs with Bingo panting in her wake. She found Mrs Beasley in a small sitting room, lying on an old-fashioned chaise longue. 'Please excuse me if I don't rise,' she said, pleasantly enough.

'I tried to stop her, Auntie, but she would come!' Bingo whined.

'That's quite all right, dear, but as it happens I'm glad that Nurse is here. I wish to discuss something with her. Women's troubles. There are some things that I cannot bring myself to say in front of a man, so if you don't mind I must ask you to run along now.'

'I can't allow that, Auntie,' Bingo said, to Maudie's surprise. 'Miss Rouse is only a nurse. If you need to speak to somebody I shall telephone Dr Dean and request a house call.'

Maudie could have sworn that a look of intense fear flashed through Mrs Beasley's eyes. 'As a midwife I do happen to know quite a bit about female complaints,' she told him. 'I shall do a preliminary examination and if I feel it necessary I shall refer Mrs Beasley to Dr Dean.'

Bingo made no move to leave, which struck Maudie as very odd indeed. Something was wrong. She knew it by the odd shiver that went up her neck, but what should her next move be? With him standing like a stone sphinx between her and the door she was sure that if she made a dash for it she'd have no chance of success.

She noticed a tall screen in one corner of the room. Made of wicker with picture panels inside the frame, it was the sort of thing that people used in draughty rooms to protect themselves from currents of cold air. Marching over to it, she managed to manhandle it to the couch where Mrs Beasley reclined, panting slightly as a result of the exertion.

Bingo looked on, making no move to assist. Maudie went to Mrs Beasley's side. 'Now then, Mrs Beasley. What is it that's worrying you?'

'I don't want to say with him listening,' Mrs Beasley mumbled. 'It's too personal.'

Maudie put her head around the screen. 'Would you mind moving back, Mr Munroe? Or better still, leave the room altogether? This conversation is between me and my patient.'

'I don't want you whispering in there,'

he growled. 'Plotting behind my back!'

Seriously alarmed, Maudie withdrew her head. Frowning and mouthing a question, she watched while Mrs Beasley nodded in response, silently jabbing a finger in the direction of the screen that separated them from her nephew.

'Have you found a lump somewhere?' Maudie asked, at the same time gesticulating and waving a thumb over her shoulder in the direction of the hovering Bingo.

'Yes,' Mrs Beasley whimpered. She drew her forefinger across her throat in a gesture that even a child could understand. 'Do something!' she mouthed. 'He's going to kill us!'

'What's going on in there?' Bingo roared. 'Stop that whispering. I can't hear what you're saying!'

'For goodness sake, Mr Munroe!' Maudie snapped, coming round the screen to face him. 'Can't you mind your own business for once? Your aunt is trying to tell me her symptoms so I can decide whether to call the doctor. I must ask you to let me carry on with this consultation in peace.'

She understood that Mrs Beasley's reply had nothing to do with lumps found on her person or otherwise. Obviously terrified, she had responded to the nurse's silent query about her nephew, and now Maudie's heart was thumping painfully as she considered their plight. The housekeeper wasn't at home and nobody else was within earshot. They were two helpless women, alone in a house with a killer.

29

'Hello,' Mrs Blunt said, smiling at the man standing on her doorstep. 'It's Mr Greene, isn't it? Can I help you? Or shall I call the vicar?'

'I'm looking for the nurse, but she's nowhere to be found. I've tried her office in the parish hall, and I've been to her place and rung and rung, but there's no answer.'

'What seems to be the trouble, Mr Greene? Is there something I can do? I have taken classes in first aid and I may be able to deal with this if you've had a minor accident.'

'It's the wife. Says she's having pains.'

Mrs Blunt recalled that Cynthia Greene, a thin, pale woman in her thirties, was expecting their first child. She screwed up her face in an effort to remember. 'But she's not due yet, is she?'

'Not for another six weeks. That's if that nurse knows what she's talking about.

Our old doctor said one thing and the nurse says something else. I wish they'd make up their minds. They're supposed to be the experts, aren't they?'

'Nurse Rouse is an expert in matters of childbirth,' Mrs Blunt told him, in defence of her friend. 'If she says that Mrs Greene isn't due for another six weeks then I'm sure she knows what she's talking about.'

'Right, then. No need to worry yet awhile. I'll go home and tell Cynthia she must be having a bit of wind or that. I'll mix her up a dose of bicarb. That should settle her.' He turned to leave.

'No, Mr Greene, wait! You may be right, of course you could, but this simply must be looked into. The baby might be coming before its time, you see. If you don't get hold of the nurse immediately, both mother and child could be in grave danger.'

'Oh, heck! What am I going to do?'

'When I spoke to Nurse Rouse earlier she mentioned that she'd be going to see Mrs Beasley.'

'Her up at the big house?'

'That's right. Look, you come inside, Mr Greene, and I'll try telephoning.'

Leaving the expectant father in the kitchen, she disappeared into the hall, where the telephone was situated. After a time she returned, her face grave. 'There's no answer at the house, Mr Greene. I've tried the surgery as well, just in case Nurse was there, but there's still no reply. Of course, it's such lovely weather they could be sitting inside, where they can't hear the phone ringing. Mrs Beasley has some lovely flower borders and she does love to show them to visitors.'

Jason Greene fiddled with his cap, which he held tightly in his beefy red hands. 'I don't rightly know what to do, missus. Reckon I should send for that Dr Dean?'

'I think you should go up to the big house and see if you can find Nurse. I can't think where else she might be. Perhaps she's already on her road home and you'll meet her on the way. Do you have transport?'

'My old truck is outside. It should take me as far as the estate.'

'Right then. Off you go, and good luck. Do give my regards to your wife.'

* * *

Mrs Beasley swung her feet onto the floor, heaving herself into an upright position. In response to Bingo's curt order, Maudie sat down beside her patient and waited for him to speak again.

'You think you're so clever, don't you, Nurse Rouse?' he sneered. 'Coming up to the surgery, throwing your weight around as if you know more than I do. What gives you the right to do that, eh? Telling me to get out while you were getting up to who-knows-what behind my back? Well, answer me, woman! Don't sit there like a stuffed dummy!'

'Brian! Don't speak to Nurse like that,' Mrs Beasley said. 'She was assigned to come here by Dr Dean, and I for one am grateful that the practice is being kept open while Leonard is away.'

'Dear Leonard won't care a hoot about his precious practice when he's rotting in the condemned cell, Aunt Cora!'

'Don't say that, Brian,' she pleaded. 'My nephew is innocent of that poor girl's death, and you know it.'

He laughed — a mirthless sound that chilled Maudie to the bone. 'One nephew, anyway,' he said, twisting his hands this way and that to study his fingernails.

'You did it, didn't you!' Maudie blurted. 'You're the one who killed Paula Mason!'

Bingo smiled.' How clever of you to work that out, Nurse. Perhaps there is a brain in that head of yours after all.'

'But you didn't mean to, did you, dear?' Mrs Beasley sobbed. 'Tell me that things just got out of hand and you didn't kill that poor girl on purpose.'

'So that's what you think, is it? Poor old Brian; everyone knows he's good for nothing. Can't get a job, can't get a girl, while smarmy Cousin Leonard cops the lot. Well, for your information, I made up my mind to get rid of that girl. She had it coming. I planned it all like a military campaign and I carried it through. It all worked like a dream.'

'How did you do it?' Maudie asked.

Bingo smiled again, a dreamy smile that spoke volumes as to his state of mind. 'She was desperate to get her precious Lenny to love her, you see. I told her I'd talked to him and made him see that she was the right wife for him. I gave her a note I'd typed up, saying it was a message from him, telling her to meet him at the hut. Like a fool, she fell for it. She was so excited, dancing around like a silly girl, telling me she'd known all along that he'd come round. It was just a matter of time.'

'And when she went there she found you instead.'

'Of course. I had my story all ready. I told her he'd been seeing a girl from Midvale and they were going to be married. That was what he was coming to tell her, only he'd been called out to a patient at the last moment and had asked me to let her know.'

'Is he really engaged to someone from Midvale?' Cora quavered.

Bingo turned on her. 'Of course not, you fool. I made that up. Anyway, she started to cry and swear. I took her in my arms and told her not to waste her tears on him; he wasn't worth it. Besides, she hadn't come all this way for nothing. She could have me instead.' His face contorted while he seemed to be replaying the scene in his mind. 'I told her I'd loved her almost all my life, ever since we were teenagers playing rounders on the common together. I've never thought of another woman in that way, never pictured myself married to anyone but her. I'd make her forget Leonard if she'd only give me the chance, I told her.

'Do you know what she said to me then? Can you guess? 'I wouldn't marry you if you were the last person on earth, Bingo Munroe!' she said. 'Look at you, you long streak of nothing! You're only half a man, if that! No girl in her right mind would come near you with a ten-foot pole! Run home and sponge off Auntie, why don't you? It's all you're good for!''

'I'm so sorry, dear,' Cora Beasley murmured. 'So you lost control and lashed out at her.'

'Oh no, Aunt Cora. I was prepared for that, you see. I had a heavy hammer in my pocket that I'd taken from your tool shed. I've put it back in its proper place there now.'

'Then you planned to kill her all along,' Maudie said.

'Yes, but I went there prepared to give her a chance. If she'd agreed to go out with me, to let us get to know each other with a view to marriage at a later date, I'd have let her live. I did love her, you see — so very much. But she sealed her own death warrant by talking the way she did.' He glanced at his aunt, and then at Maudie. 'Just as you two have sealed yours,' he said, pulling out a gun.

'Where did that come from?' Cora bleated.

'Souvenir of the war. I'm an old soldier, remember?'

'You won't get away with this,' Maudie told him.

'You think not, Nurse? I've given the housekeeper a week off to visit her sister in Morecambe. I'll be long gone before she comes back and discovers the bodies.' He pointed the gun at Maudie.

She closed her eyes. *Where are you, Dick? Where are you when I need you?* But Dick was far away in Canada, and he could not come to the rescue. Well, if she had to die, then her last thoughts should be of him, and perhaps somehow her spirit would reach him to say goodbye. 'I love you Dick,' she murmured.

30

A thunderous knocking could be heard somewhere down below. Maudie's eyes flew open. Gun in hand, Bingo turned to face the door, listening intently. Maudie bit her lip. Was there a chance that she could catch him off guard, knock the firearm to the floor and snatch it up before he had time to retrieve it?

But what if she did? Would she dare to pull the trigger? She knew nothing about guns. She might do the wrong thing, leaving herself and Mrs Beasley even more vulnerable. She had been hoping for a quick, clean death, over with before she realised what was happening. If he was sufficiently maddened he might make them suffer before they died.

The knocking continued. 'Nurse! Nurse! Are you in there? I need you to come with me. It's the wife!'

'Up here! I'm up here!' she bawled, before Bingo had time to stop her. If he

264

killed her now the police would at least know who had done it, and he would be brought to justice.

In a flash Bingo ran to the open window, clambered onto the sill and teetered for a long moment. Then he was gone. Rushing to the window, Maudie saw him racing across the lawn, limping badly. He must have fallen awkwardly, but otherwise he seemed unhurt. Dr Lennox's car was parked on the gravel drive and he wrenched the door open and threw himself inside. Moments later they heard the car start up and he was gone. The key must have been left in the ignition, she thought.

The knocking and the shouting continued. Maudie took Mrs Beasley by the arm. 'I have to go. It sounds as if someone's in trouble. You'll have to come with me.'

'No, I don't think so,' Mrs Beasley faltered, but Maudie had no time to waste in argument.

'I'll take you to Mrs Blunt. You'll be safe there. Where's your handbag? Bring it with you and let's go.'

'There you are, Nurse! I thought you were never coming!' Jason Greene, his hair awry, greeted Maudie indignantly. 'It's our Cynthia. She's having pains, she says, and she wants you to take a look at her. And what's the matter with that chap? He drove out of here like a bat out of hell, just missing my truck by inches!'

'We've had a bit of trouble,' Maudie told him, 'but it's all sorted now, or it will be when we've had a chat with the police. I'm ready to come with you now, if you wouldn't mind putting my bike in the back. And we'll drop Mrs Beasley off at the rectory on the way, and after that I'll have to pop in at home to pick up my bag.'

Within minutes they were on their way, all three of them squashed into the cab of Jason's old truck. Maudie spoke firmly to Mrs Beasley, who was visibly shaken.

'You must ask the vicar to telephone the police immediately. Don't do it yourself because they might not believe you, after your little, um, mix-up with them before. I take it you know the license plate number of Dr Lennox's car?

They'll need that if they set up roadblocks to try to catch Mr Munroe. And you keep your mind on the road, Mr Greene,' she went on, seeing that he was looking at the pair of them open-mouthed. 'It won't help your wife if you land us in the ditch.'

'But what's he done, Nurse?'

'I'm afraid I can't discuss that now, Mr Greene. You'll have to wait and read about it in the *Chronicle*.'

'Oh, the shame of it!' Mrs Beasley wailed. Maudie could have kicked herself. She had meant her comment as a little joke to throw Jason off the scent. Now she had managed to upset Cora Beasley even more than she already was. As for the publicity that was sure to come, that could hardly be worse than what the poor woman had already suffered.

A short while later she escorted the shivering woman to the front door of the rectory. Mrs Blunt answered at once and helped to bundle their parishioner inside. 'Can't stop,' Maudie gasped. 'Got a patient to see to. Please get the vicar to send for the police at once. It's extremely urgent. Mrs Beasley will tell you all about it.'

★ ★ ★

Cynthia Greene was hunched over in pain when Maudie bounded up the stairs of their little brick semi. 'It's coming, Nurse. The baby's coming, and it's weeks too early. Am I going to lose it? I can't bear it, Nurse. We've waited so long for this baby. Please tell me it's not going to die!'

'I'm here now, Mrs Greene. Let's get you up on the bed, shall we? You give me a hand here, Mr Greene, will you? Yes, that's right.'

Maudie confirmed that her patient was indeed in labour, and that everything was progressing normally.

'Now you're here I think I'll go down the Royal Oak,' Jason said. 'I'll only be in the way if I stay here.'

'If I might have a word with you, Mr Greene? Outside, please.' Usually she was glad enough to see the back of expectant fathers, but this case was different. She followed him onto the landing, closing the bedroom door behind her. 'I want you to stay in the house in case I need to send you to phone for an ambulance.'

His eyes widened. 'Is there something wrong with our Cynthia, Nurse? Back in there you told us everything was normal. She'll be all right, won't she?'

'As I said, her labour is progressing nicely. I have every reason to expect that all will be well. However, the baby is likely to be rather small, and in need of specialised care in a hospital setting. We shall have to wait and see.' She returned to the bedroom.

Mrs Greene was not yet fully dilated and she seemed cheerful enough. Maudie checked her blood pressure and listened to the baby's heart rate, and all appeared well. She drew up a chair and prepared to wait.

★ ★ ★

Some hours later a baby girl slid into the world, wrinkled and completely bald. 'She's so beautiful,' Cynthia breathed when her daughter was placed in her arms for the first time. 'Isn't she the most beautiful baby you've ever seen, Nurse?'

'Of course she is,' Maudie agreed, privately thinking that the poor little scrap had a face that only a mother could love. Of course, that would change in time. She chuckled, remembering another baby she'd delivered recently. When the baby boy had been shown to his big brother, the four-year-old had howled in terror. 'They've pulled out all his hair and teeth!' he'd complained. Maudie still wondered who he'd thought responsible for this heinous act, but who knew what got into the minds of small children? It was beyond her understanding.

The Greenes were saddened to learn that their little girl was being sent to the cottage hospital, but they accepted Maudie's gentle explanation with good grace. Little Rose had been born too soon and needed to be in an incubator, where she would receive oxygen until her little lungs had finished developing.

'That's why I want her to go by ambulance,' Maudie went on, when Jason insisted that he wanted to drive the baby to the hospital himself. 'They'll be able to start giving her oxygen right away in the ambulance. And besides, she's too little to be able to stand being jostled in your truck.'

Cynthia looked sadly at the first-sized baby clothes, so lovingly prepared, that were far too big for her daughter.

'You'll be able to dress her in those when you go to fetch her home,' Maudie told her. 'By then she'll have put on a bit of weight.'

By using the kitchen scales, Maudie had learned that the child weighed four pounds, eight ounces. 'Newborns usually lose a bit, so Rose will probably drop back a little more over the next few days,' she went on.

'Isn't that dangerous?' Cynthia looked alarmed.

'Do try not to worry, Mrs Greene. She'll be properly cared for by the nurses at the cottage hospital, and by the time they've brought her weight up to five pounds she'll probably be ready to come home.'

Maudie waited until she had seen little

Rose safely into the ambulance and then she took her leave of the new parents, promising to return the next day to check on Cynthia. She hoped that all would go well with the child; neither Maudie nor Cynthia could think of any reason why the pregnancy had ended early. Perhaps Rose's early arrival was just one of those things. Whatever the cause, it had probably saved Maudie's life, and probably that of Mrs Beasley, too. There had been no time to dwell on it before, but now the whole nasty episode came flooding back, and she suddenly felt quite ill.

Dismounting from her bicycle, she leaned over a nearby privet hedge and was thoroughly sick into someone's herbaceous border.

31

The next morning Maudie received a phone call from Mrs Blunt. 'How are you feeling after all the excitement, Nurse?'

'Quite well, thank you. Mrs Greene had an uncomplicated delivery and the baby girl is in satisfactory condition in the cottage hospital.'

Mrs Blunt laughed. I wasn't talking about that! I have every confidence in your skills as a midwife.'

'I suppose you mean that business with Bingo Munroe. I'll feel a good deal better once I know he's safely behind bars, preferably in a mental institution. And I'd give a lot to know why he did what he did.'

'That's why I'm calling. Mrs Beasley would like you to come to tea today. She's staying with us because she really wasn't fit to be at home alone, especially with her nephew still at large. She has things she wishes to tell us, and Harold thought it best if we all came together to hear. She's already been through it once at the police station, and the poor woman is quite worn out. Shall we say three o'clock?'

'Can I bring anything?'

'No, no. I've made a cherry cake and a few egg sandwiches.'

'Right, then. I'll see you later.'

'I look forward to it.'

★　★　★

Dressed in a rose-pink linen frock and white sandals, Maudie started out for the rectory in good time for the tea party. A black car was drawn up at the gate and she felt a pang, imagining that Dick had driven it there. But when she was shown into the rectory drawing room she found a detective in plain clothes and a uniformed policewoman, neither of them known to her.

Mrs Beasley was sitting upright on a sofa, well in control, yet very pale and seemingly somewhat shrunken. The vicar and Mrs Blunt were the only other people in the room. Mrs Blunt began passing teacups to the visitors while her husband, well used to chairing parish meetings, opened the proceedings.

'Since you were present at the, er, incident yesterday, Mr Maxwell here would like to hear your version of events, to see if it coincides with what Mrs Beasley has told us.'

'It isn't that we disbelieve Mrs Beasley,' Maxwell said, which Maudie thought was handsome considering the way the older woman had tried to bamboozle the police earlier on. 'It is a known fact that when several people witness a certain event and are questioned about it later, there are as many versions reported as there are observers. To your knowledge, did Munroe have a weapon about him yesterday?'

'I should jolly well think he did!' Maudie told him. 'He was armed with a gun.'

'What sort of gun was it?'

'I have no idea. I'm not an expert on guns. All I know is that it was a souvenir of the war; at least, that's what he told us.'

'And you believed he might use it?'

'He certainly told us that was what he meant to do! I thought my last moment had come. And if it hadn't been for the fact that a patient's husband came looking for me there, I doubt if I'd be sitting here drinking tea with you today.'

'Quite so. Now this is important, Nurse Rouse. Did Munroe make any sort of confession in your hearing regarding the death of Miss Paula Mason?'

'Yes, he did. He said he'd planned to do away with her because she'd rejected him, and he lured her to the hut for the express purpose of killing her.' Maudie glanced at Mrs Beasley, who had her eyes closed. A solitary tear ran down the lined and papery cheek.

'I see. I think that will be all we require, Nurse, except that you may like to know the outcome of yesterday's incident. Mrs Beasley and the vicar have already been informed of this. Brian Munro was found dead in the early hours of this morning. He had driven his car into a stone wall surrounding the old livery stable at the Spread Eagle at Midvale. He is believed to have been killed outright.'

'Oh, dear,' she said, feeling inadequate. There wasn't much else she could say with the man's aunt sitting right there. He was her flesh and blood after all. The detective and his silent driver left then, leaving Maudie with a good many unanswered questions.

'Are you all right, Mrs Beasley?'

'I suppose I should be asking you the same thing, dear. After all, you could have been killed, and by a member of my family, too.'

'It was lucky for both of us that Jason Greene turned up when he did. I've never thought of him as a Galahad, but he was certainly in the right place at the right time. What happens to Dr Lennox now, Mrs Beasley?'

'Oh, he's been exonerated completely, of course.'

'And will he be returning to Llandyfan soon?'

'Apparently not. He has agreed to stay on for a while to help those poor sick men.'

'I feel he is wise to do so,' the vicar observed. 'All this business will be a nine days' wonder. He should perhaps stay out of the limelight until all this dies down.'

Maudie thought that it would take a good deal longer than nine days for Llandyfan to settle down again, but she said nothing.

Mrs Blunt hesitated before joining the conversation. 'Did the reason behind this murder have something to do with unrequited love? I understand that Mr Munroe carried a torch for the young woman for years. So when she wanted nothing to do with him, he decided that if he couldn't have her, nobody else should. Is that what it was all about?'

'I'm afraid it was rather more than that, Mrs Blunt. Brian thought of himself as a poor relation, which I suppose he was in a way. Even as a boy he was quite jealous of Leonard, or Leo as his own parents called him. I think Brian could have made something of himself if he'd made up his mind to try, but that wasn't in his nature. When things went wrong it was always someone else's fault. When Leo got into medical school, it wasn't fair. The whole world seemed to be against poor Brian.'

'There are some people like that,' the vicar noted.

'Then the war came and Brian got called up and, like thousands of others, he had to serve in the army,' said Mrs Beasley. 'Leo was permitted to stay on at medical school, supposedly because the government wanted as many doctors as the medical schools could churn out. After all, none of us knew how long the wretched war would last, did we?'

'But he survived the war,' Maudie said, 'and I know there were government schemes afterwards for veterans to attend college and take up their education where they left off. Surely Bingo — er, I mean Brian — could have taken advantage of that? He might even have become a doctor himself.'

'What you don't know, my dear, is that Brian spent some time in a mental hospital after he was demobbed. The doctors said that the terrible things he had seen had affected his brain. They called it shell shock in the Great War, didn't they? Perhaps they have a different label for it now. Eventually he was discharged, but in my opinion he was never really fit to function like other men. He's never been able to hold down a job for long, you see. He always had some excuse; people didn't like him, or the bosses were against him. That sort of thing.

'Then his mother died and he was alone in the world. He came to me from time to time looking for money, and I did oblige him for a long while, until Leo pointed out that as long as Brian had me to lean on he would never pull himself together and try to make a go of things. And that made sense to me, so I cut back on what I'd been doing for him.'

'And I doubt if that endeared Dr Lennox to him either,' Maudie said, earning a slight frown from Mrs Blunt. Mrs Beasley turned to Maudie with a nod.

'That is exactly right, my dear. Before you turned up yesterday, poor Brian confessed it all to me. He deliberately set up a plan to lay the blame on Leo for the killing of Miss Mason.'

Mrs Blunt gasped.

'Oh yes, Mrs Blunt; I know what you must be thinking. Brian was evil. Yes, it would have been truly evil to let Leo go to the gallows, but as I've said, Brian wasn't in his right mind. It's my belief he should never have been discharged from that place, but there are so many poor souls in far worse condition that the doctors cannot help them all.'

'What about the letter?' Maudie asked.

'Which one are you referring to?'

'Was there more than one, then?'

'Oh, yes, and he typed them up on the machine in the gatehouse. He sent one to the newspaper, pretending that Miss Mason had written it as a plea to Leo; and the other, of course, he used to lure the girl to the woodcutter's hut, where he killed her.'

Her three listeners fell silent, contemplating the implications of Mrs Beasley's story. Still overwhelmed by the realisation of her narrow escape, Maudie asked herself whether she was a meddlesome fool who had walked straight into a dangerous situation, and was lucky to be alive. If, on the other hand, she had minded her own business and not gone to talk to Mrs Beasley, that lady could well be lying dead in her own home at this very moment, with nobody any the wiser. For having told his story, would Bingo have allowed his aunt to go on living? Perhaps he would have shot her and then gathered up any valuables kept in the house, and gone abroad. Yes, it was rather nice to think of herself in the role of guardian angel!

She stared at the Blunts, trying to gauge what they were thinking from the expressions on their faces. Soft-hearted Mrs Blunt had her eyes shut and her lips were moving silently. Praying, Maudie decided; perhaps trying to intervene for Bingo, who had had such a difficult life.

The vicar's expression was stern. Maudie had heard it said that he believed in the existence of Satan in the world. Did he suspect Bingo of having aligned himself with the devil? Maudie would have given much to know, but she dared not ask.

'I don't believe he committed suicide, you know,' Mrs Beasley remarked suddenly.

'You mean Mr Munroe?'

'Brian, yes. I think it was the car that caused his death. It wasn't his, you see, and I don't think he understood how to drive it. He never had one of his own; he couldn't afford to run one. He often told me that. Hinting that I should give him one as a present, you see. Of course, he may have learned when he was in the army. Still, the car crashed when he was running away, but I'm sure he didn't do it on purpose.'

'I expect you're right,' Maudie told her softly. If the poor woman derived some comfort from thinking that her nephew's life had been taken in an accident rather than by suicide, one could only be glad for her.

32

September. After a week of wet weather, during which rain had dripped constantly from the roof of Maudie's cottage, leaving pools of water everywhere, Nature had relented. From her bedroom window she could see mist rising in the fields beyond the village, a sign of a fine day to come.

Thankful to have a day off at last, she strolled outside and set up a deck chair in the shade. She meant to spend the morning reading, or simply doing nothing at all. Recently there had been too much anxiety, too much striving. She needed to find an oasis of calm.

The year was passing quickly and it would soon be harvest time. In another month Dick would be home, and she wondered how their reunion would be. Would they be stiff and awkward together after their long separation, or would they slip into their old, comfortable relationship as if they had never been apart?

Until recently Dick had written faithfully, but his letters had been most unsatisfactory. Yes, he had laboured to give an account of his life in Canada, but he had never responded to her many questions, and there had been no words of love. Was she expecting too much? Not everyone was a natural writer, and emotional outpouring was not Dick's style.

Yet they were not an old married couple! She needed a bit of romance in her life. *Forget about that now, Maudie,* she told herself. *Dwelling on what you can't have won't do you any good.*

She leaned back in her chair, trying to recall the words of a poem they'd learned at school: 'To Autumn', by John Keats. According to their teacher he was one of England's greatest poets, yet the poor boy had died at the age of twenty-six. What might he have achieved if he'd lived to grow old? Or would his talent have gone off the boil, rubbed out by life's hardships and disappointments?

'Season of rain and mellow fruitfulness,' she quoted aloud. 'Close something of the something sun.' No, that wasn't right. 'Season of mists and what?'

'Close bosom friend of the maturing sun,' a well-remembered voice said in her ear. Was she hallucinating? She swung round suddenly, almost collapsing her rickety deck chair.

'We had that poem at school too,' Dick said. 'I've never been quite sure what it all meant.'

Maudie leapt up, almost knocking him off balance. 'Steady on, old girl,' he warned. 'Mind my arm!' She saw then that he had his arm in a sling.

'But it's only September,' she babbled. 'And what have you done to yourself? And look at you; your face is all brown. Are you sure you haven't been to Africa?'

He grinned. 'How about some breakfast for a hungry man? I've been travelling all night and I had to do the last bit on the milk train. I've not had a bite to eat since yesterday dinnertime. You do me a nice fry up and then I'll tell you all my news.'

Maudie was suddenly aware of her appearance, dressed as she was in a faded cotton frock, with bare legs above ancient sandals. After washing her face that morning she hadn't bothered to put any lipstick on, and now she felt dowdy and unkempt.

'I could do you a couple of poached eggs on toast,' she suggested, thinking to take refuge in everyday tasks to help her overcome her shyness.

'Or fried eggs on fried bread, with lashings of HP sauce,' he said. 'Three fried eggs would be lovely, if you can spare them.'

* * *

'Now then, Dick Bryant!' Maudie exclaimed, when he had rather awkwardly wiped his plate clean with a slice of toast in order to retrieve the last trace of egg. 'What are you doing here? What happened to you? Why didn't you let me know you were coming?'

'Whoa, steady on! One thing at a time, old girl. I had an accident and broke my arm, and with this plaster cast getting in the way I wasn't much use to them on the job. There wasn't much point in going on sick leave for weeks when I was in another country, so when they offered to send me home early I jumped at the chance. I didn't write and tell you because I wanted it to be a surprise.'

'It certainly is that! But how did you manage to break your arm?'

He shrugged. 'I had a little argument with a mad bull.'

'What!'

'We — my partner Shane Rawlings and I — were called out to a farm by a distraught woman whose little girl had been cornered by a bull. The child had been warned to stay away from the animal but she'd gone into the field with it because, as she told us later, she wanted to give it a bunch of clover as a treat.'

'Never mind the clover! What did you do?'

'I just slipped inside the rails and snatched up the kiddie, and passed her over to Shane. The bull charged and I managed to flip myself over the fence in the nick of time. Unfortunately I landed on this arm, and the rest is history.'

'And you could have been history, too! Or you might have been gored!'

Dick shrugged. 'Well, I wasn't. And what was I supposed to do, stand there and watch while that toddler was maimed or killed before my eyes? Forget all that! Fill me in with what's been happening here. Have they got to the bottom of that murder yet? Did your Dr Lennox kill the girl after all?'

'I wrote and told you all about it!' Maudie said indignantly.' Didn't you get my letter?'

'No, I didn't. I've been traveling around quite a bit on the job, and of course I've been at sea for the past week. I suppose your letter will catch up with me eventually, if anyone bothers to forward it. Now then, if you've got another deck chair, let's go back outside, and you can tell me who dunnit!'

Sitting outside in the sunshine, Maudie filled him in on the details of the murder, glossing over her own narrow escape in the process.

'What about Dr Lennox, then? Do you think he'll come back here and start up in practice again?' Dick wondered.

'I really don't know. The last I heard, Mrs Beasley was talking about selling up and moving to a retirement home in Devon. I suppose they could sever the piece of land the gatehouse is on, but I don't know if people would feel comfortable going to poor Dr Lennox now. You know what people are like. No smoke without fire, they'll say, that sort of thing. If I were him I'd go somewhere far away and start afresh.'

'Mm. And speaking of fresh starts, now that I'm back we'll have to get busy with our wedding plans. We can bring them forward now, if you don't object to seeing me waiting for you at the altar with this thing on my arm.'

'There's one thing I want to know before we get into all that.'

'Oh, yes?'

'How are Ruthie's boils? Are they better yet?'

Dick stared. 'Maudie Rouse! What on earth are you talking about?'

'You sent me a photo of yourself with someone called Ruthie hanging around our neck. You looked like you were having a jolly good time, too!'

He blushed slightly. 'Oh, that was Shane's wife, just clowning around. He was taking snaps and told her to get in the picture with me. That's all it was.'

'Oh.'

'But what's all this about boils?'

'It was written on the back of the snap: 'Ruthie, Corn boil'.'

Dick began to laugh. 'You'll be the death of me, Maudie! Over there a corn boil is an outdoor party when they cook cobs of corn over a fire, roll them in butter and salt, and eat them while everyone stands around talking and singing.'

'Corn?'

'Yes, you know, maize as we call it here, only not the stuff you feed to cattle. It's an edible variety. Sweetcorn, they call it.'

'Ugh! It must be an acquired taste. Did you enjoy it?' But a loud snore was all that greeted her question. Exhausted, Dick had dropped off to sleep.

Maudie sat back, feeling more contented than she had for a long time. All was right with her world now that her beloved Dick was by her side. She began to count her blessings. All her babies had come safely into the world. Little Rose Greene had come home from hospital and was thriving.

Now that the shadow of Paula Mason's murder had been lifted, life was good for Maudie's friends and neighbours as well. Johnny Grayson had started life at the grammar school, wearing a second-hand uniform and, wonder of wonders, his lazy father had actually landed a job on a building site. Just how long that might last was anyone's guess, but with any luck his wife, Rita, would keep his nose to the grindstone.

And speaking of wives, poor old Fred Miller would have to give up the notion of taking Maudie to wife as the comfort of his old age, but he'd get over it. Maudie looked at Dick with affection.

Dear old friend! He might be a hopeless correspondent, but he had proved himself to be brave as a lion in the defence of a Canadian toddler. How grateful that child's mother must be feeing now!

And Maudie was grateful too. Thankful

beyond measure that Dick had been given to her, and happy in the thought that they would go forward into a new life together, to live as one until death did them part.

She looked up at the sky. 'Thank you!' she murmured to whoever might be listening up there.

'Wassat?' Dick mumbled.

'Nothing, dear. Go to sleep. God's in his heaven, and all's right with the world.'

THE END

We do hope that you have enjoyed reading this large print book.

Did you know that all of our titles are available for purchase?

We publish a wide range of high quality large print books including:
Romances, Mysteries, Classics
General Fiction
Non Fiction and Westerns

Special interest titles available in large print are:
The Little Oxford Dictionary
Music Book, Song Book
Hymn Book, Service Book

Also available from us courtesy of Oxford University Press:
Young Readers' Dictionary
(large print edition)
Young Readers' Thesaurus
(large print edition)

For further information or a free brochure, please contact us at:
Ulverscroft Large Print Books Ltd.,
The Green, Bradgate Road, Anstey,
Leicester, LE7 7FU, England.
Tel: (00 44) **0116 236 4325**
Fax: (00 44) **0116 234 0205**

Other titles in the
Linford Mystery Library:

THE CHAINED MAN
AND OTHER STORIES

Gerald Verner

When a band of stranded Christmas travellers is forced to spend the night in an isolated local pub called the Chained Man, the last thing they expect is murder in their midst . . . Lattimer Shrive puts his amazing powers of detection and deduction to work to solve three seemingly inexplicable cases . . . And a real murder on national radio proves surprisingly tricky to solve. These five detective stories by Gerald Verner will baffle and entertain in equal measure.

THE DARCKMOOR DEMON AND OTHER ENIGMAS

John Light

Who or what is responsible for the eerie howling from the night-darkened fells that disturbs the inhabitants of Darckmoor? Is there malice at work in the world of small presses? Why is there an eight-foot-high toadstool on the back of a truck speeding along a remote byway? When a new statue by a reclusive artist is displayed in a small gallery in London's East End, is it the beginning of something bigger? And what is the cause of the sorrowful single-mindedness of the long-term resident of an old-fashioned hotel?

FIRE IN THE BLOOD

Rena George

Gennie Durham buys into the Flying Fox country pub, and finds herself in the middle of a Yorkshire murder mystery — with Oliver Hammond, the man she is becoming increasingly attracted to, as the prime suspect. But there's worse to come . . . An arsonist is on the loose in Fenwick-cum-Marton. The historic St Stephen's Church has already been burned to the ground. Is Gennie's pub next on the fire-raiser's list?

MOON GARDEN

V. J. Banis

After recovering from a nervous breakdown, Ellen comes to her aunt Minna's Southern mansion to regain her strength, but strange events begin to haunt her. She glimpses people in various places, only to be told by those people that they had never been there; when they also deny the reality of other things Ellen claims to have seen, she is forced to consider whether her illness is returning to poison her thoughts. Only when a woman she has seen is found murdered, does Ellen finally realise the terrifying truth . . .